A GUEST HOUSE IN AZ ZUBAYR
Inspired by a true story

by

Brian Godfrey

*To Mary
much love.
Brian G.*

Published by New Generation Publishing in 2021

Copyright © Brian Godfrey 2021

First Edition

The author asserts the moral right under the Copyright, Designs and Patents Act 1988 to be identified as the author of this work.

All Rights reserved. No part of this publication may be reproduced, stored in a retrieval system or transmitted, in any form or by any means without the prior consent of the author, nor be otherwise circulated in any form of binding or cover other than that which it is published and without a similar condition being imposed on the subsequent purchaser.

ISBN
  Paperback   978-1-80031-040-7
  Hardback   978-1-80031-039-1

www.newgeneration-publishing.com

Foreword

A difference of opinion.

Two of the most prominent religions in the world have a divide in their followers.

The differences occurred long ago, but the discrepancies are still standing with Catholics who did not follow the King's wishes in the sixteenth century were ostracised, and the Muslim faith was split by the bickering when trying to agree the method in selecting a new Caliph.

In the world today, the majority of countries strive for peace. It is an expectancy of the human race, to always hope that the wars and turmoil of the past are just a passing shadow, but they never are. Even in the world of divine faiths, there are differences that continue to blot the civilised world.

The Catholic Pope as an example built on the rock set by St Peter in Rome and is the leader of over billion Catholic followers, but in the sixteenth century, when Henry VIII suggested he break one of the rules by asking the Pope for a divorce, he was refused. As a consequence, he started his own church, one that would allow personal freedoms, like allowing the divorce he wanted for himself.

Islam had a major dispute early in their history, and the outcome left their believers in disarray. The argument stemmed from the method that was proposed to nominate a new Caliph, and the problem between Sunnis' and Shias' still exists to this day.

The disagreement over the nomination arose when some followers claimed the Caliph should be nominated democratically, and others believed it should be decided by inheritance.

Iran-Iraq conflict, 1980–1988

There are many reasons why Saddam Hussein invaded Iran in 1980. One of these reasons was the personal hatred between the new Iranian leader – Ayatollah Khomeini – and Saddam Hussein, and another reason was the differences regarding the Muslim factions – with Hussein being a Sunni and Khomeini being a Shia.

Throughout his reign, Hussein was prejudiced against the Shias. He continued to persecute them throughout the war, and the majority of his Command council was made up mainly of his own sect: Sunni Muslim.

Chapter 1

The Dark Side of Paris

13th June 1980.

She looked exquisite walking down General de Gaulle's Boulevard. She had beauty and flare, and was doing her best to show it off.

Maria was a working girl and business had not been good during the winter, but now that spring had arrived and the sun was shining, she was hoping for a good year. Her money was running low, and with a family to keep in Orleans, it was necessary for her to keep earning. She worked continuously in order to pay the bills for her five-year-old son, but she was missing him immensely and was desperate to return home.

The previous night, sitting at the bar at the Meridian, a hotel in the centre of Paris, she was approached a man. He was casually dressed in light blue shirt and white trousers, his body was slim and athletic, but his face was lined, probably from the sun. He seemed troubled by something and she had a feeling she would soon to find out.

His face was expressionless when he approached her, "Bonjour Madame, je m'appelle Criff. Can we chat for a moment?" She smiled back and nodded for him to proceed. She assumed at this stage that he knew she was a working girl.

He looked around to ensure no one was in earshot, and was very direct. He spoke in a low tone, and after a few sentences she became aware that this was no ordinary proposal, nor was this an ordinary man.

"I want you to do something for me in which you will be paid generously," he paused to see her reaction.

"And that is?"

"That is to make 'friends' with a man that I will identify in due course."

"And then what?"

"I want you to seduce him and allow me to get access to his room." He studied her face intently.

"That sounds normal, do you want to hurt him?"

"Not necessarily, we only want information."

"That will cost you $2,000. American." She knew her price.

"Too much. $1,000 plus what he pays."

"OK, let's do it. But 50% up front and the rest afterwards."

"That's fine. We will meet here tomorrow, but make sure that you come… prepared." With that, he smiled for the first time.

Then he added, "Please be discreet and under no circumstances will you mention our discussions with anyone, and I mean anyone."

She smiled at him and was attracted to his slim muscular body. His face was quite gaunt and often expressionless. Only when he smiled did he become a different man, but this was never for long.

"I understand," she replied.

"This is just a simple task, Maria, and if you are interested, I will meet you in the hotel tomorrow at three thirty – and please, this is our secret."

"You said here, did you mean in the bar or the foyer?" she queried.

"The foyer, but if you're under this roof, I will find you."

That evening Maria slept well. She was excited about the promise of work and the money Criff had offered her.

The next day.

Maria was awake early and made up to look as beautiful as possible, without looking garish. It was as though it was a type of business meeting she was attending and not her normal type of work.

The walk took her no more than twenty minutes and she soon reached the hotel, breezing into the foyer as if she owned it. The hotel was her 'office,' she came in every day and knew it well. She took a seat close to the entrance, so she could recognise the man she had met the previous day, and just three minutes past the half hour he walked into the hotel. He looked handsome, with a deep tan that emphasised his sexuality. For a second, she thought of herself as a woman, and then turned her mind quickly to the matter in hand.

He recognised her, but his face did not show this, it remained passive as he did not want to draw attention to himself, and he slid discreetly into the seat next to where she was sitting.

"Bonjour Maria, I am glad that you are on time, perhaps you will join me for a walk, and we can discuss our business in confidence, or maybe stop for a coffee if you'd prefer."

After walking for a few minutes, he spoke in a low voice.

"A man will walk through the door of the Meridian in an hour. His name is Dr Yahya Mesad and he will go straight to the bar and order a drink. You will make friends with him and, depending on your prowess, suggest at the earliest convenience that you will go with him to his room."

"Is that all? That is just my normal business," she laughed.

"That's right, but when you are ready to leave you will telephone me with the pretence of phoning for a taxi, it is then that I will enter his room, as I have some business with him." He paused and looked at the Maria. "Do you understand?"

"Are you going to kill him?" she asked.

"I need to talk with him, purely business."

She thought long and hard, "OK, but the price has doubled, and as agreed I will need to be paid half now and half after I have done my part."

He handed her an envelope, then from his pocket he counted another five hundred dollars and added that to the envelope.

"OK then, we have a deal. One thousand now, and the rest tomorrow. I will phone and tell you directions for where to meet. Please give me your phone number."

The next day, 17:00hrs.

A taxi crawled along the Champs Elyse, with two passengers in the backseat. They were speaking in Egyptian and were in deep conversation.

Returning to their hotels after a hard day's work at the French nuclear Institution, the older and more senior official was Dr Yahya Mesad, a nuclear physicist working on a reactor owned by the Iraqi government, the other was his assistant, Abdul al-Rasoul.

Dr Mesad was talking about terrorist acts that had blighted his life, "You know Abdul, I was happy in Egypt when I was working with the Egyptian Nuclear Program, but it was short lived. As you know, it was bombed by the British during the Suez Canal crisis, and now we have the same situation occurring under our noses here."

"You mean the threats?"

"Absolutely! None of this fills me with confidence."

"And *this* is?" Abdul asked innocently.

"It is due to the anger of the Israelis. They're becoming nervous of the Arab countries and our progress in developing nuclear facilities, especially with our clients, because the Iraqi nuclear development is improving and is becoming a danger."

"And you think a bombing will occur again?"

Mesad paused and sighed "I hope not. This is our future, my friend."

The car soon approached Abdul's place, and he exited the car in his usual spot.

"Good night, sir."

"Good night Abdul, inshallah."

The taxi continued to the Meridian, and at half past six, Mesad entered the foyer and walked to the bar where he ordered a soda water with lime and ice. He drank a third of the glass in one breath, as it tasted especially good on such an unusually hot day.

"Now, that looks an excellent choice in this weather," Maria broke the man's concentration.

He looked at who had spoken and immediately smiled. She was extremely attractive. "Yes, that was nice." He answered in broken French, but in no time at all they were talking as if they had known each other for years.

"Now, my dear lady, I am going back to my room to freshen up and it would be my pleasure that you accompany me… we can talk business on the way."

One hour later.

Maria stirred in the large bed, untangled her legs from his and quietly slipped away in an effort not to disturb his sleep.

Earlier she had noticed a telephone in the bathroom, so the rest was easy for her once the door was closed.

"My name is Maria, I am in room 1016, can you pick me up at the Hotel Meridian in five minutes?" She put the phone down.

She dressed and waited just inside the door waiting for contact with Criff. In no more than three minutes, there was a tap on the door.

As she left the room, Criff and another man entered.

She did not want to be seen, so she skipped quickly along the corridor, and used the stairs to get out of the hotel. It was nice to breathe in the fresh spring air.

Inside the room, the two men moved quietly but efficiently, one went into the bathroom and started to wipe clean all surfaces that Maria may have touched. His accomplice walked over to the bed with a small pickaxe in his hand, similar to those used by skiers.

As he approached, the physicist suddenly looked up, bewildered. The man brought down the pickaxe on his head, crushing it with one blow, and he fell back onto the pillow.

Criff looked over to his accomplice and whispered, "It would have been better with the pillow – but it is done, let's go. I will continue to check for anything that may arouse clues to us or the girl being here, and you, pack your bag."

The attacker put the pickaxe into the backpack he was wearing, and then moved to the door and waited.

Criff opened the door ajar, and ensuring that it was clear, slipped from the room. Five minutes later, his companion followed him, and they exited the hotel quickly.

The following morning.

Mesad's assistant, Abdul, waited for his boss at the pick-up point for an hour but it was in vain. On returning to his hotel, he telephoned the Meridian, the receptionist told him that Dr Mesad had not been seen, she thought he was sleeping but said she would check.

It was four hours later that two policemen visited Abdul at his hotel and told him of Mesad's death. They informed him of the brutal murder and reassured him that they were investigating the circumstances.

Abdul immediately phoned his client and requested a flight home to Cairo. He would, before his departure, make out a full report and deliver it to his Iraqi director.

Two days before he was due to leave, he attended a dinner with his business colleagues. After the meal and immediately after the coffee, he made his excuses and left the restaurant.

It was only a short distance to his accommodation, so he decided to walk. At the first road crossing, he waited for the pedestrian green light, then started to walk briskly across the road. After just a few yards, a speeding car that hit him before he had reached the safety of the adjacent pavement. Abdul was knocked high into the air before hitting the road with a thud. He died on impact. And even though the street and shop lights were at full blaze, the police found no witnesses.

*****

Maria was angry at Criff. He had not contacted her as promised, and it was now three days since the incident, and his debt to her was still outstanding.

On the fourth day she received a call from him, he said he would meet her on the north side of the Luxemburg Gardens opposite the hotel Angelina in Paris.

He gave her full instructions, and she needed to wait only one more day to get her money, she was looking forward to going home.

Maria was nervous with the publicity, and the police investigations. They were getting closer to her and claimed she was seen in the hotel on the day of the murder.

With these implications, the situation had worsened, the Parisian newspapers were continuing their interests of the physicist's death, and things were becoming an International hot topic.

However, she felt better after speaking with Criff and would travel immediately to receive her payment from him at a pre-determined rendezvous and then leave for her home in Orleans.

A day later, Maria was walking north along the perimeter of the Luxemburg Gardens, it was a warm night, and she was a few minutes early, so she did not rush. Soon she was in sight of the hotel, but she stopped and waited for an oncoming car that was travelling at speed to pass, but as she did the lights of the car blinded her and a few seconds later hit her at high speed. She died on impact and the street was deserted with no witnesses.

June 1981

The death of the three innocent people was investigated for many months after the fact, but the French police found so many blind allies during their investigation, it seemed there were no witnesses and no clues to work on. The case continued loose the spotlight and interest dwindled, the police realised they could go no further and left it unsolved, but open.

On the political front, the death of Dr Mesad was a serious blow to the Iraqi Nuclear program, and things got worse when the Israelis made a surprise air strike code named 'Babylon', on the 7th June 1981. The raid made by a squadron of F-15As, destroyed the facilities at Osirak.

This offensive used Mark 84 bombs, which were dropped in pairs at five second intervals, with half of the sixteen bombs dropped hitting their target.

The reactor core was destroyed, and for a long time so was the Iraqi Nuclear weapons program.

Chapter 2

Arrival in Baghdad

July 1983.

Baghdad International Airport was abuzz when Ed Copping disembarked the plane. It was not crowded with military personnel, as one would expect during a war, but with a well-dressed assortment of passengers, predominantly of male gender. Some were dressed in western lounge suits, others in classic Arabic dish dash. They all looked incredibly well-to-do, certainly not what you would expect at such a crucial time in Iraqi history.

Whilst waiting in line to pass the border security, Copping needed to be calm, there was still some way to go until he reached the desk, this gave him the opportunity to assess the attitude of the border control officers.

Normally their demeanour is non-committal, a job carried out in normal circumstances would be routine, but in wartime attitudes change. They were now on high alert, and more aggressive than normal. He waited patiently, rehearsing how he would deal with the situation when he came face to face with his appraiser.

His nerves were fraying waiting in line, his heart was thumping, his hands shook uncontrollably. *Keep focused, pull yourself together, take a deep breath*, he thought to himself. It was simple; just keep a cool head and look bored, that was it. He examined the attitude of the officers and there were no niceties exchanged with passengers, their attention to detail was precise, and they seem to take forever to carry out their tasks. They were leaving no stone unturned and were checking that passports were legitimate, checking visas for authenticity, facial checks against ID photographs, there were no exceptions. Their tenacity put him on edge. Iraq was no place to end up inside of a prison cell.

It was getting to the end of the line and he needed to be positive. With nowhere to turn, he tried to re-align himself, turn his mind onto better things, getting apprehended now was not an option.

A few minutes later he handed his documentation to the officer, trying to act normal. Without more than a glance, an officer took his passport and documentation and checked them meticulously. After three long minutes – it felt more like three hours – the man stamped his papers and handed them back to him. Without haste, Copping started to walk away from the booth. He reminded himself that he must keep calm and slowed his movements, while making his way toward the exit. It felt better with the gate in sight, and in a moment, it was over and he felt relieved. His arrival procedure had gone smoothly. Now happier, he headed to collect his baggage.

The place was mobbed, with many passengers milling around the carousel, all jockeying for position. They looked bad tempered as he tried to push through, but those standing in a waiting position made it difficult. Eventually, he decided to wait and found a space to linger.

After half an hour, the baggage started to flow. It seemed like forever, but soon his bags were in site and his worries were over for the moment, and he headed for the arrivals lounge.

The noise of the taxi drivers hit him hard, all of them scrambling for a good position, and each one trying to be louder than the next. The situation transcended down the line of drivers, about thirty of them were all waving a paper in the air, each with the client's name on it. It was difficult for the passengers, who needed to decipher the jumble of Arabic/English letters that were scrawled on the paper. Copping tried to read the names on the sheet, but as quickly as he focused on one sign, the paper moved. It was impossible to even vaguely make out, they had all been illegibly scrawled. It seemed these guys wanted business so badly they would take anyone for a price. But then he heard a familiar name, and it was repeated.

"You Mr Copen?"

"Yes, I'm Mr Copen." While he rudely mimicked the man, he was relieved that he at least had a ride, he hoped safely, into town. After all, one thing was certain, he needed to get away from this madhouse.

"I take you to hotel."

A few minutes later he was on the road from the airport, and along the newly constructed highway, traffic flowed quickly. However, damage from a recent Iranian air attack was still evident. The narrowing of the road eventually slowed the traffic, and the idea of queuing seemed to incense the drivers, but once they passed the obstruction they took off at breakneck speed. Their only thought was to get the next fare as soon as possible.

The size of the posters along the highway depicting Saddam Hussein in various poses amazed Ed, not so much the content but the size. This huge billboard appeared to run along the ten miles into the city, dominating the scenery. It seemed to him that the Ba'ath party did not want anyone to forget who was running the country.

It was apparent that Saddam Hussein needed publicity, as he was not a local – but a native from Tikrit, a town situated about a hundred miles North of Baghdad – he was also a Sunni Muslim, and in the minority.

The taxi soon reached the built-up area on the outskirts of the city, and the cab swung around into the access road next to the Meridian hotel. As he disembarked from the cab, he could not help but to notice the huge statue of Saddam that dominated the Firdos area, the President was in your face in every direction. He shrugged it off.

Approaching the receptionist, Copping was relieved that she spoke excellent English.

"I want to check in, but first I would like to know the price per night at your best rates." He was nervous in case in he did not have enough cash on him.

"Your name, sir?"

"Edward Copping."

"Have you got a reservation, sir?" the receptionist asked.

"No," replied Ed.

She hammered the keys of her computer, then after studying the screen for a few moments, looked towards him. She spoke in a clear but slightly affective accent. "It seems, sir, that you are already checked in, and your account has been paid for the next week."

"Booked in and paid by whom?" Copping queried.

"That I do not know, but if you can fill in this card while I prepare your welcome package."

He entered the open lift a few minutes later and it whisked him up the inside of the hotel foyer. The lift's sides were glass, with a view of those below, and soon the lower floor of the hotel disappeared.

In his room he raided the complementary fridge, he was so hungry after the journey, and scoffed as much of the snack food as he could. It had been some time since he had eaten, and he was not sure if he could afford dinner later.

He soon felt better and turned his attention to other things. Carefully, he unscrewed the heels from the main body of his shoes and removed the remaining bank notes that were stuffed inside. He felt remorse as he counted it, only a few dollars remaining. It was important for him now to find a way to release other funds from his small reserve he had hidden in England. He needed someone who he could trust.

Now feeling tired, he thought this problem would look better after a sleep, and so he collapsed onto the large armchair, and turned on the TV. It was CNN and Becky Anderson was talking about the world, he did not last long and soon fell into slumber. However, it wasn't long before the ring of his room telephone woke him with a start.

"Hello, Copping here."

"Is that Barney?" a gruff, Irish voice at the other end of the line asked.

His mind was fogged and he waited holding in his breath. Who would know his history? A few seconds passed, "I don't know a Barney. My name is Edward!"

"OK, OK cut the bullshit, I know the situation… uh… Mr Ed, so let's get that straight," said the voice.

The caller paused, he was aware that the telephone was probably tapped, a method that the Iraqi secret service used on many expatriates living in Baghdad. He did not want to pursue this line of conversation. A lull transpired while he collected his thoughts.

"My name is O'Byrne and I plan to visit you in an hour, please meet me in the hotel lobby. I will have a blue suit with a red tie. Be punctual."

"What do you want to discuss, Mr O'Byrne?"

"We can discuss that in an hour." The line went dead. O'Byrne was very abrupt and Copping was coming to his senses very quickly, especially after hearing the name O'Byrne. It was the same name of the man that was his boss in Shetland. This man was an IRA commander.

He thought for a few moments and shook his head. *No, this must be a coincidence. It's just two people with the same name, surely that's not possible.* The O'Byrne he knew previously was an IRA commander, but was apprehended and reportedly died in Moscow.

*****

"Mr O'Byrne?"

Ed had identified the only man in the foyer wearing a tie.

"Yes, it is." He stood, they shook hands, and O'Byrne gestured to a vacant chair adjacent to him.

"Thank you," said Ed, who sat down, waiting for O'Byrne to start proceedings.

"You do not know me but you may have heard of me. For a short while I was your commander, after you were recruited and sent to Shetland."

He stopped and waited for Copping to respond.

"Well yes, I was confused," he looked more closely, "what happened?" He paused, then spoke again before O'Byrne could get a word in.

"Did the police release you after the debacle at Glasgow airport? I heard that you went to Russia."

O'Byrne smiled, "Yes, the British police, bless them. They couldn't hold me, lack of evidence and all that." After a while, he continued.

"I was remanded in custody by the police for a time, but was later released, it was too late then to get involved with the assassination attempt." Pausing then added "A bit disappointing that the attack failed in the Shetlands, but it's all history now!"

He did not mention his own reported death, and after some thought added, "Later, I was called to Moscow to complete my training."

"Your training in Moscow, what was that all about?" Copping seemed astonished.

"Don't look so surprised, Mr Copping. I now work for the KGB, and unless you want to return to Ireland, then you must now realise that you do too."

"I do, since when?"

"Since you left Zambia in a hurry, with the authorities close behind." O'Byrne laughed.

There was silence between the two, as Copping was trying to come to terms with what O'Byrne was saying. He felt uncomfortable and realised that he was being coerced into working for the Soviets.

"Have I got a choice?"

"Probably not, unless you want to go to prison."

"How long have you been tracking me, Michael, if I may call you that?"

"You know, Copping, that we have people all over the world doing what I do for my adopted country, and yes feel free to speak your mind."

"Which country is that, Mr O'Byrne?"

"The one that pays my wages, same as you."

"Was it George Mwanza who informed on me?"

"Mr Copping, there are no comments and no personal questions, it is in the past."

"Mr O'Byrne, are you controlling me in the job that I have been offered?"

"Not directly, you provide me with information when I ask, but you will be working for a man that I went to college with, in Moscow. He is now Assistant Director General of construction at the Iraqi Petroleum institute."

"I assume that I get paid, or am I a slave to the system?"

"Of course you get paid for the work during the day, but not for the information that you may get for me, that is my pay back. Now, if there are no more questions, just enjoy the hotel and I will be in touch with you soon. You will require terms and conditions, a work permit and living allowance. I will provide these in the next day or so, and by the way, you will be paid monthly."

O'Byrne stood up, waited for Copping to do the same, they shook hands again, and he left the hotel.

*****

Copping spent his first two nights moping about the hotel, feeling unsettled about venturing outside. It was his opinion that a foreigner from the west, exploring a city that was currently at war, would not be welcomed with open arms. O'Byrne had warned him that all foreigners are classed as spies by the ruling Iraqi Ba'ath party.

He was also concerned about his financial state, as he had little funds with him, and it would be a month before he was paid his first salary. The funds that he had started with when he left Zambia had now dried up. He wanted access to his savings that were stored in the UK, but getting them would be difficult. He thought of Martin Valeron, a man whom he had known since working in the Shetland, and whom he had met again in Zambia. Copping thought at one time he might well have been the one that exposed him, but things had changed. He felt he could count on him as a friend, a person to trust. Copping was aware that Martin would not be in Zambia forever, he would return sometime soon to the UK, and if he was to ask him to access the funds and credit an account here in Baghdad, it would solve his immediate problem.

On the third day of just surviving around the hotel, he decided to venture outside and explore the city. He realised the best day to do this was Friday, the day of prayer in Islamic states, as it would be quieter and more suitable for exploring.

Chapter 3

River Tigris

August 1983.

Copping studied the layout of the city and knew from the tourist map the river Tigris flowed to the east from where he was staying. He would need to consult a map and plot his route carefully. It would be a disaster if he got lost in Baghdad and picked up by the police, and this was easily done, so he worked out a simple route that would direct him in a circle.

He remembered that O'Byrne had advised him that he should not talk with any Iraqi people outside of work, nor should he mix or socialise with the local people, unless they were directly associated with him in business.

With this mandate, it was unlikely that anyone would be sympathetic to a lost foreign soul wandering around the centre of the city if he stopped to ask the way in a foreign language.

He estimated the walk would take an hour and decided that he would log his movements on a map. He had noticed that all the major roads were labelled in English as well as Arabic.

Turn left at Firdos Square, at the river turn right, walk along the far side of the river, turn right again at the fourth bridge, immediately over the bridge take a right along Rashid Street back to the hotel.

Once out in the hot sunshine, he kept left and continued down the slope until he reached the river. Turning right, he found a gravel path on the left side and keeping alongside the water's edge, he carefully counted each of the bridges as he passed them. Once he had reached the fourth one, he crossed it, and started the circuit back to the hotel.

The air was unnaturally calm, with no wind and little noise. A few people were in the vicinity, but it seemed to Copping that something was not right, the place felt eerie. His concentration was suddenly broken when he noticed some activity on the banks of the river, a few hundred yards away. He continued walking and reached the centre of the bridge, stopping to look around the surrounding area. He was startled by loud thudding-like noises coming from the far bank of the river. It was close to where he had spotted some activity only minutes before, when crossing the bridge. It was a sound that he thought resembled automatic rifle fire. He thought it was military manoeuvres, so he re-positioned himself for a closer look to see what was going on.

The noise stopped. Then he heard sharp instructions from a voice shouting in Arabic. The whole situation made him feel uneasy, but still he moved position again to get a better view. He soon recognised that it was soldiers carrying guns, and was surprised they were firing so close to the city.

He continued to walk along the bridge pathway, even more nervous now, as something told him this was the wrong place to be. He slowed his walk, stopping briefly to look back. He felt nauseas at the sight before him, he realised an execution was about to take place on the banks of the Tigris, and he could do nothing about it.

The shots rang out again, echoing off of the local buildings. Crack! Crack! Crack! The noise bounced back and forth from houses close by, and the retort impaired his hearing.

Straining forwards and focussing his eyes, he recognised what looked like four bundles on the sand. Even from a distance, Copping realised they were bodies, and looming over them were a group of soldiers dressed in uniform, holding rifles.

He maintained his gaze and watched as the bodies were removed, and another four men were led onto the sand and left to stand. More shots rang out and the men fell to the ground. He looked away, knowing he had seen something that he should not have. He felt exposed, and what made him feel worse was some local people were standing on the opposite side of the road, they also looked uncomfortable, and a few were looking across the river in the direction of the shots. Some looked across at Ed, and he felt as though he were intruding, and felt he must get away quickly. This situation was private to the Iraqi people, it had nothing to do with him and it was a terrible thing for him to have witnessed. He wished the ground would consume him, as his mind wondered to the victim's families. How deep was their anguish and grief? Did they witness the killings or were they soon to hear about their loss?

To him it was a personnel shock but to the victims' families it would certainly be devastating! Feeling sick, he turned and strode away from the scene, re-tracking his steps. In less than half an hour, he walked through the lobby of the hotel and headed straight for his room, where he threw himself into the bathroom and was violently sick.

Later that day he still felt at a loss, his mind was drowning in empathy for the relatives of those shot in full view of the city. He recapped the situation: who were the soldiers that died? Were they the enemy or fellow Iraqis who committed treason?

Perhaps they simply spoke out against the Ba'ath party, or were from the Shia sector, or were soldiers thought to be agitators. Either way, an example was made of them.

He had read in the English newspaper issued in Baghdad, that there was a militia made up of Iraq Shias who were fighting for the Iranians and operated in southern Iraq near to the Shatt al Arab. This army were brave but treasonable. In any case, he wanted to find out how and why these assassinations took place, it may keep him alive in the future.

Trying to sleep and forget the day's incident was impossible. Copping tossed and turned, and finally awoke. It was late afternoon, and he needed to get out of his room, so a few minutes later he made his way to the bar on the first floor. He needed to get out and find a way to raise his spirits after his experience.

The lobby was busy, he saw there were four or five groups of westerners chatting in various areas of the adjoining foyer.

He did not know anyone, so he walked boldly towards the service area, where he intended to order a drink.

Two younger men were standing to his left as he approached the bar, they were discussing something in an unfamiliar language, and on his right side sat a lone westerner. This man was dressed in grey slacks, a blue lightweight jacket and an open necked shirt, with his black hair swept back at the sides, and a glass of beer and a book in front of him. It seemed to Copping that the man was totally oblivious to what was going on around him. He was to find out later that it was just the opposite; this man was subtly observing everything in his immediate vicinity.

Approaching close to where the man was seated, Copping tried to catch the barman's attention, but it seemed he was busy serving others. Ed, in trying to maintain his composure, moved closer to the man reading his book.

Perhaps it was too obvious that Copping was lonely, as he felt uneasy, then he finally caught the barman's eyes and ordered a drink.

Suddenly, the man looked up from his book, and with the utmost panache, coolly greeted the Irishman. "Good evening," said the westerner, speaking in almost perfect English, curbed only by a hint of a continental accent.

Ed smiled back and blurted out, "My hotel room is just too small, after a while it becomes just too claustrophobic, so I had to get out."

"That, my friend, is why I am here reading my book here at the bar. But first, may I introduce myself? My name is Jean Paul Krull. Call me JP."

"And mine is Edward Copping, call me Ed." They shook hands.

"Of course, dear boy."

Over the next two hours, the men had become firm friends. They did not seem to notice that the two younger men, who were chatting opposite them, were constantly trying to muscle in on their conversation, but they had too much to talk about between them, and so ignored them.

JP did at one time acknowledgement them with a nod, and as he turned away to break the ash from the cigarette, he squeezed his foot gently onto Ed's shoe. The point was made, and both kept silent.

After a few minutes, the two younger men left the bar, smiling and politely waving goodbye as they headed towards the door.

For a while there was silence between the two, then JP looked down at the ground and quietly said to Ed, "The two men were speaking in Hebrew when I arrived, I suspect them to be Israeli secret service from Mossad, they're always meddling around here in the bar, looking for any information regarding the military."

"The intelligence side of the Ba'ath party are also in here often, so always be careful of what and who you speak with. You never know, and one mistake may be your last!"

"How do you know this?" asked Ed.

"I speak five languages fluently, including Arabic, but I have not told anyone else since I arrived here, until now. I would appreciate if this remains that way, you understand."

"Of course, thank you, JP."

Chapter 4

The Iraq-Iran War

1980–1988.

In September 1980, Iraq invaded Iran. This was at a time when the Iranians were at their most vulnerable following a civil war. The Shah of Persia was deposed, and the country was now run by the Islamic cleric, Ayatollah Khomeini. He was the founder of the Islamic Republic of Iran, and this would change the Iranian political hierarchy forever.

Saddam was of the opinion that success over Iran would make him the supreme leader of the Arabs, and the expected success over the Iranians further boosted his already large ego. The oil wells that he expected to capture would only feed his appetite to buy more arms.

At first, the Iraqis crushed the hapless and brave, but ineffective, Iranian army. Hordes of young men carrying inept weapons were killed in thousands. Initially, the Iraqis enjoyed the fruits of war by capturing men, Iranian ground, and oil wells, but the Iranians regrouped and retaliated by sending thousands of soldiers into battle in a human wave. The Iranian army had a resolve, a term that the Iraqis did not possess, and they were driven back to their borders.

Life was relinquished, with multiple casualties on both sides. The stench of war reeked in the areas of combat, where the fallen were left to steam in the hot midday sun.

The Iraqis held the military power, with their Russian MIG fighters controlling the skies, and it was becoming a desperate situation for the Iranians who did not know where they were to get the financial support they needed.

Then, out of the blue, came an unexpected saviour, it was an offer they could not refuse, even if it came from Israel a most hated enemy, the deal would prove to suit them both.

With the state of Israel surrounded by a host of Arab nations, there was no room for respite, their army was always on high alert and their intelligence service working behind the lines to support 'The Knesset,' Israel's parliament.

If Israel were to survive, they would need to negate any aggression from the Arab nations close by, and if by chance a deal was on the table from one of them that would be beneficial without potential risk, they would take it!

As Iraq continued to pursue nuclear development, Israel saw this as unnecessary aggression that threatened the safety of their people and using carefully selected intelligence, they retaliated by first eliminating Iraq's leading scientists and then destroying their nuclear research centre at Osirak.

The Israelis actions were an agitation for Saddam, he would stop at nothing to succeed in building weapons big and powerful enough to destroy his enemies, and to do this he would need to use unconventional weapons that were banned by international humanitarian law. These laws, established by an international committee and influenced by the Red Cross, differentiate conventional weapons, from weapons of mass destruction (WMD).

The three main variants of the outlawed weapons (WMD) are classed as nuclear, biological or radiological, and it seems are supplied by the same countries that set the ban in the first place.

The war between Iraq and Iran continued to swing first one way and then the other, and after four years it was in a stalemate. When either of the combatants had the advantage then the other would retaliate with some form of unconventional force, and with each action then many thousands were killed.

*****

August–September 1983

The Iranians, now emboldened by their deal with Israel, were restocking their armaments, and among the weapons purchased were a number of scud missiles from Libya, which had adequate range to reach Baghdad.

The first attacks hit the city randomly, and the first explosion gave a warning to the people of Iraq that their war was to become more personable. The bombing had a demoralising effect, and they braced themselves for the next explosion, not knowing when and where it would occur.

Within a twenty-day period, two scuds hit Baghdad. One fell on the north side, destroying a bakery, and the other fell close to the river, again on the north side but with minimal damage and no fatalities.

A group of visiting businessmen were in a hotel on the North side of the city at the time and were disturbed that they were so close to the missile explosion.

One minute they were relaxing in the clubs, then the blast hit. It was enough to cause the most severe anxiety. The noises, dust and panic that followed made them realise it was time to live outside the killing zone. At first it was an inconvenience but one they found necessary to follow if they were to survive.

But the expatriates found that things were not the same and although some stayed away in safe areas, the more hardened moved back to the city after they heard that Copping had developed a system that predicted where the danger existed every day.

Copping was intrigued by the way these missiles were deployed. At first, he thought it was by remote control, but then he found out that these scuds were not a smart design, they were genetic the same as the basic rocket that De Braun designed nearly forty years prior. They simply dropped to the ground when the fuel ran out.

Ed studied the pattern of attacks each night and compared them with a number of variable aspects.

The Iraqi press at one time predicted where the launch was made in Iran, so Copping checked with his own basis of analysis and found little difference in the predictions.

During his calculations, he tried to take all the variables into account, such as the time it took to load and launch the missiles on site. He would then make duration allowances for things such as storage, transport, installation, hook up and launch. With each of these plotted sequentially, he then came up with an estimated time the missiles would be launched.

The Iranians did not have unlimited missiles, and the probability was not to launch more than one a night, and the one they did launch would need the right weather conditions to favour a hit in the centre of Baghdad. And Copping's calculations indicated when these conditions were suitable.

He now refined his plan, utilising all available technical data, such as deviation in flight, density of air, drag, wind speed, missile weight and water. Then using the manufacturers data, such as take-off, cruising speed, normal operating range, turning rate etc. He could then predict an approximate position of danger in Baghdad.

By producing a simple vector diagram on a local city map, for each night he could estimate where the next missile would land, and this was what the expatriate community put the faith in.

More by luck than by judgement, his prophecies proved reasonably accurate and it gave immense satisfaction to the marauding westerners who once again could socialise in the hotels with some confidence, based on Copping's calculations.

His reputation began to proceed him, as each evening information was spread around the expatriate community. The calculations were not correct by the minute, but they were good enough to warn the others when and where they would be vulnerable, and they followed his advice with confidence.

During his socialising, they became aware of Copping's endeavours, and many made satirical comments behind his back. The first attack after he produced the curves came ten days later, the missile did not kill or destroy, but came within eighty metres of his prediction.

Thirteen days later, another scud made a direct hit on a small hotel on the north side of the river and was much closer to the heart of the city. This time his prediction showed the result was only fifty metres off of its target.

Copping's scientific approach was basic, but he was happy it was working. Many new visitors to Baghdad heard of his prophesies and put them to the test.

But this was a dangerous game, and members of the MI6 British Intelligence service who were based in Baghdad heard about his map. A report of their findings was soon sent to London addressed to Tom Patten, the project manager, and the person in charge of Edward Copping.

This directive is with regard to your employee, a Mr Copping, who is issuing detrimental information to British expatriates in Baghdad. He should be instructed, with immediate effect, to stop any further work on this issue and have all subsequent plans and calculations confiscated.

We would expect you, as his company's senior representative, to surrender this information to the SIS offices in London in the next five days, and in no circumstances should any further work proceed on this issue, nor should any copies of the said report exist. All copies should be immediately confiscated, and the circulation of anything of this type will be deemed illegal from this date.

Should this situation continue or be repeated in any form, we will need to pursue the matter further with the source.

Signed,
The Director of Middle Eastern Operations

Patten was annoyed. This man that he had never met, who was technically working for him, needed to be reprimanded. Any suspicion that was on Copping would be a reflection on his company. Patten would telephone him to get his story first, then make a decision!

In the meantime, Copping had become even more popular with the foreign community, and had taken up the responsibility of managing reservations for the Meridian tennis court, the only court south of the Tigris. Expatriates from the western world visiting Baghdad for business, or seeking a recreational facility, telephoned Copping requesting a game. The situation became hectic, with Copping arranging games for independent people covering a time period from five until ten o'clock every evening.

He was receiving faxes and telephone calls from all over the world. This was unpaid social work outside of his normal day job, however the information he was compiling filled up his journals that O'Byrne required from him.

Diligently he kept a record for each person that played, and it was O'Byrne's tactic to randomly request information, without warning.

Whenever possible, Copping obtained a calling card from the person playing, which he used to later verify their authenticity.

He carried out traceability exercises for each person, matching the information on calling cards with what they told him. When it didn't match, he passed this onto O'Byrne.

Ed had to analyse every word that was said, and when the person was not fluent in English, it was necessary to decipher it before handing them over to O'Byrne.

The information that he thought useful was normally snippets of personnel information: company addresses, travel details, local contacts and their business in Iraq.

It would allow him to deduce if they were legitimate visitors and if there was any doubt in their integrity, and O'Byrne could make a more in-depth evaluation utilising the KGB intelligence system.

A few weeks earlier, Copping had joined the British Club, which was purely an institution that provided social activities for expatriates.

During one of his visits, he noticed a poster on the entrance board, asking members to sign up for a four-way game tournament that was to be arranged between employees of other expatriate company's working in Baghdad. The categories of competition involved cricket, athletics, darts, and snooker, and the participating companies that were to enter the competition included a construction company, Indian employment agency, Irish Health company and the British club.

He entered his name to be considered for selection, and a few days later attended a meeting at the British Club and to find out what it was all about.

*****

Copping's professional boss was Tom Patten, and the two were expected to meet in the forthcoming week as Patten was to travel to Baghdad in a day or so.

Copping's working terms and conditions at the Petroleum Institute were a complicated arrangement, and this situation could only have transpired in the way that it did due to the inability of Patten to recruit in London. It seemed British personnel did want to work in a country at war.

It was only for simplicity that Maliki, the Iraqi Project manager, suggested a local hire, and Patten agreed. However, since the episode with the SIS regarding Ed Copping, who was tracking scud missiles, he was now having second thoughts.

Patten was in the mood to travel and was looking forward to witnessing the start of construction, he could clear up any design problems, and utilise the visit to interview Copping.

In Baghdad, Copping had already signed his contract with Mr Mahmoud, the Institute's construction director, but reading his work brief he found his responsibilities were wide ranging.

He was to monitor four separate projects and produce detailed reports on planning, estimating, and cost control.

The compilations of the projects were interesting, as the design and procurement activities were virtually complete, which left the emphasis on construction and commissioning.

Patten was only responsible for design and procurement, but he was looking forward to the construction and commission phases to ensure it complied fully with his company's design.

But his visits soon become tedious, a string of engineering problems, endless contractual queries, and personnel irritations. It all started with Copping, who was deliberately putting other ex-patriots in harm's way by advising them where to avoid missiles. The one thing that Patten did not want on his CV were the deaths of those given miscalculated advice by one of his employees.

And the last thing that Copping wanted was to give the impression that he was spending more time organising tennis than he was doing his work.

Copping's initiation into the Petroleum Institute came shortly after he had signed his work contract, and one of his first duties was to attend a 'kick of' meeting with the Iraqi construction team.

Those that attended included the Iraqi project manager, Mr al-Maliki (project manager), Mr Mahmoud (construction director), Mr Gorges al-Mubarak (design director), and a surly man called Mr Gharlib al-Sadr (party member).

Also in attendance was the Engineering manager, an Armenian called Alex Magarian. He was a slim, good-looking man, dressed immaculately in a grey suit. He had thinning hair, small features and bright clear eyes, and his appearance gave one the opinion that he was from a high class of upbringing, and his impeccable English practically confirmed it.

Although the director was at the top of this hierarchy, each of the five projects had a project manager that was in charge of day-to-day operations, and the fifth project was of a classified nature.

All had graduated from western universities and spoke the language of the country they had studied, and English as a matter of course.

One of Copping's duties was to chair a bi-weekly progress meeting for each of the projects, and that included all five-project managers. Neither Mahmoud nor his deputy attended these, but they always diligently studied the minutes when they were issued a day later.

The schedule for the main project, the southern export lines, was delayed due to design amendments, and as a consequence both Patten and Copping would be under attack from the Iraqi management. Inevitably, this would result in a confrontation with Mahmoud.

Patten's visit would give him the opportunity to brief Copping, as he had already had discussions with the two new construction superintendents back in London, and this would be one thing less for him to be concerned about at least.

It would also give him the opportunity to meet the whole team at the Institute.

The role of chairman went to the project director, Ahmed al-Maliki. He was a short man, in his late sixties, his hair had almost gone and the few strands that remained were swept back over his head. But he did have tremendous magnetism, and it was difficult to be sure whether it was his huge eyes that never seemed to blink, or the impression that his mind was calculating some complicated mathematical equation in his head. He was renowned by other members at the Institute for being remarkably astute, and today he looked incredibly dapper. He was dressed in a smart dark blue suit and a colourful tie, he spoke excellent English, and unlike Mahmoud who was sitting next to him, he was gentle and reserved.

However, behind this, he possessed a steely mind that would evaluate a conversation in seconds, interject where necessary and change the bias of the discussion to his own requirements. He was not the sort of person you would want on the other side of the table at a contracts meeting.

Mahmoud, the construction director, was of a different nature. Despite being older, he was still large and boisterous. Now, in his late fifty's, he could take over a meeting with his intimidating voice, that reverberated around the room when he spoke, and he made no excuses if he verbally attacked anyone that crossed him.

Unlike Maliki and Magarian, he was not a dapper dresser, with his light brown suits always seeming a size too large and his choosing to wear a tie only a few times a year, which showed by the clumsy way the knot was tied. In general, he was someone who looked totally uncomfortable out of his casual day-to-day clothes.

The others in the room remained inert, apart from Sadr who continually counted his worry beads and threw random questions at the meeting. Copping was of the opinion that he talked just to be noticed.

Sadr was a member of the Ba'ath intelligence section and everything that was said was reported back to his party. It was his job to shadow all foreigners at the petroleum office, including Copping and Patten, who were not trusted by the other engineers. They knew he would report anything he thought negative to his party hierarchy, this might be political comments or technical actions.

On one particular day, the meeting broke up after two hours without any issues to note. Those at the meeting, apart from Mahmoud, moved to an annex room where there was tea and snacks laid out on the table.

Copping did not say much and thought it better not to discuss anything until Patten arrived from the UK next week. So, he just listened and absorbed as much information as he could, as he knew that O'Byrne sometime or another would quiz him.

*****

Copping was looking forward to seeing his new friend JP, as he was beginning to feel low and was in need of some humour. He was sure that JP was the man to lift his spirits.

As usual, JP was sitting in his place at the bar, reading his book, as though he was oblivious to all around him. Of course, this was never the case, and Copping had already determined that this man knew, at every minute of the day, who was close and what was being said. With five languages to his name, he had the credentials to understand what was going on in an international lounge.

"Hi JP, it's good to see you here so early, I thought that I would be sitting on my own."

"Oh, hi Ed, how was your day?"

"Great, I met with the construction group that I'm going to work with and it went down well, but now I need a drink."

"Oh, by the way, the receptionist told me there's a letter or something waiting for you at the desk, so you best run along and see what it is."

"Okay, thanks, I'll be right back."

After reading the note he didn't go back to the bar, it was from O'Byrne. He left immediately, without saying goodbye to JP, deciding to apologise later. He did not like O'Byrne but thought it best to play along with him, and under no circumstances upset him at this stage. So, he made his way outside and asked the porter to order a cab.

Chapter 5

A Pub in Rashid Street

September 1980

The pub in Rashid Street was not full, although about seven or eight rough Bedouin-type characters were drinking at a table right in the centre of the pub. They looked either Turkish or, he assumed, like tribesmen from the North of Iraq. Their trousers were baggy from the knee up and two or three were armed with both knives and small pistols.

Apart from their armaments, their persona was not threatening, and Copping made for a seat in the corner of the room. A window was close to his seat and he could watch the world go by as he waited for O'Byrne.

He was jolted back to the present by a rasping voice, "You want drink, or you eat?" asked a scrawny-looking waiter that hovered close by. The man that spoke was thin, making his nose the most prominent part, it was almost to his chin. His clothes were bright and clean, but were two sizes bigger than necessary. Although his eyes glinted, his face was long and serious, as if the world were on his shoulders.

"A bottle of beer, please."

"Large or small?"

"Oh, a large one and ask my friend," he waved his hand in the direction of O'Byrne who was standing behind the waiter, trying to navigate around him to the seat opposite Copping.

He stood up and shook O'Byrne's hand and they both sat down.

O'Byrne opened the discussion. "I have been busy reviewing our situation here in Iraq, and it seems you have been diligent so far with your work, and reading the document that you sent me, you're a busy man, but you'll need to change your content into something that I can use."

"Dig a little deeper you mean?"

"Yes, I need individual intelligence regarding oil export programs, new pipelines and relevant information. It may be the case that my client requires information of any potential business opportunities, and of course any high profile purchasing that is in the pipeline. You must remember that their nuclear program is still in existence and should you hear anything, you need to let me know immediately."

There was a pause and O'Byrne looked down at his drink, he was obviously mulling over what to say next.

"By the way, there is one particular item regarding Iraq's armament program that needs to be clarified, and I will be disappointed if you cannot confirm the rumours that are circulating."

"Rumours, concerning what?" asked Copping.

"We are to understand that the Italian mafia have opened an 'office' in the Vatican and are pursuing certain nuclear materials. If this is the case, it will be necessary for us to eliminate any further development."

"How will I find out about this? It must be top secret and a million miles from my domain." Copping shook his head.

"If you want to stay and live life to the full as you are doing now, then I fully expect that you will do a full investigation on this. You have the contacts and you're in the circle of the powers that will know exactly what is going on!"

O'Byrne's eyes were like steel and they bore into Ed's, "You understand, my friend?"

"Yes."

"Then let's talk about your movements inside of the Petroleum Institute, the people that you have met, and any information that will be of interest to me."

"I will do what I can, but please be more definitive, it would help me a lot."

"Have you met your employers? And who in the hierarchy are you erh, familiar with?"

"Only project and construction manager level, I'm sorry to disappoint."

"We need to know who can be bought, you understand?"

"Well, I have met my new Iraqi employers and I am to understand that my London boss, Tom Patten, will visit next week."

"Yes, that may be a man we can deal with."

Ed looked despondent and groaned at O'Byrne.

"My main concern at the moment is money, I have debts and the hotel needs to be paid otherwise I'll be out on a limb."

O'Byrne laughed, "Don't worry, Copping, Patten will sort things out when he comes over, besides the hotel will not expect to be settled until the end of the month".

"OK, Mr O'Byrne, what else do you need, I hope that there is nobody that you want assassinated, because I am not open to that."

"Please, Please, that is going over the top, and stop referring to spy novels, keep your eyes and ears alert, that's all you need to do."

O'Byrne continued, "Do not only restrict yourself to the Sheraton and Meridian, move around other places where you can pick up information or rumours that may be circulating. You will come across certain individuals that are not here on business, but they are sometimes dangerous and can eliminate you in a minute, so be careful."

Each held their gaze on the other, then O'Byrne continued.

"Look, Coughlin, or is it Copping? We are sitting here now in the centre of Iraq, the birthplace of civilisation, and the country is at war with Iran. It is unfortunate that the two leaders representing the warring countries personally hate each other with a vengeance, but both of them are now responsible for thousands of deaths, and because of their individual ambitions, each want to be top dog here in the Middle East. It's a power struggle. Though both have a common enemy, the chosen state of Israel, and no matter how much either would like to blast the other into oblivion, which will not happen, now or in the near future. And that is why 'Mossad'," O'Byrne's way of pronouncing Mossad, "are keeping a very close eye on them. If they continue to develop anything that may jeopardise their own safety, they will strike back quickly."

"Unfortunately for them, Iraq are relying on the development of a nuclear warhead. This may be a long way off but if one of them succeed, it will destabilise the world, and destroy Israel."

"Which countries are the main players supporting Iraq's Nuclear Program?" O'Byrne took a swig of his drink. Copping was becoming very interested and knew he would need to obtain any and as much information as he could on this state of affairs.

"Most European countries are involved, with the Americans and British supplying the leading line in conventional weapons. Our main concern is the nuclear aspect."

He continued, "As I mentioned earlier, a third party may be involved illegally, possibly the Mafia or a similar organisation, who may broker a deal with a uranium supplier, possibly in Africa, procuring unregistered material. Their intentions may be to smuggle nuclear reactive materials into Iraq, because they cannot do so legally due to the Convention on Certain Weapons."

"So, you need information on how and when, I assume," said Ed.

"Exactly, but we also need to know how close the Iraqis are to producing a nuclear bomb. And we need to know what the Israelis are up to, and my opinion is that they are playing a double game."

"Double game?" Copping was confused.

"Israel are cunning, unscrupulous businessmen, so never be surprised what they might do."

"Supporting both sides in a two-way conflict, you mean?"

"Maybe. It's up to you to find that out."

There was a pause and O'Byrne went on "But be careful, these guys have ways of making people disappear."

Ed's mind began to race, but O'Byrne interrupted his thoughts by saying, "You will be busy my friend, and oh, there is one other major point of concern, I need to know why and how the Iranians are doing so well in this conflict when they would appear to have no finances, nor any international backing."

"Are the States involved?" Copping queried.

"The CIA are involved in everything, they're either stirring things up or sticking their nose in things that are none of their business. They're forever trying to cause instability in the Middle East. Nevertheless, they're a strong ally of Israel, as most of the hierarchy in Washington are Jewish, but the biggest arms supplier in the world is the US company *General Electric*. Business is business and ethics don't come into it."

O'Byrne was on a roll and continued with his lecture to his new lackey. "We also understand that China are supplying the world, since breaking out from the communist name tag, they're in it for business, they'll supply anyone."

"One last thing, Copping, you should be aware of a connection between the Iraqis and the French, they're in bed together regarding nuclear development, so anything you hear, write me a report."

The group of Bedouins at the middle table were breaking up, as they all seemed to be shouting and slapping each other. Then one of the men, the biggest of them all, suddenly drew his pistol and took a step back. Everyone in the room froze, waiting for the inevitable, when the gun sounded and the man he was threatening dropped to the floor. Both O'Byrne and Copping held their breath, but didn't dare to move, he could turn the gun on them just as easily. The big man suddenly relaxed, breaking out in laughter and fell back on his chair, stuffing the pistol into his waistcoat.

It was obviously some sort of prank, as the person on the floor got up and moved away from the main group. O'Byrne turned away, as he did not want to stare in case the tribesman turned on him, he was still unsure if the man was wounded or if it was a game.

The others now all sat down around the fat man with the pistol, he had moved from his previous seat and was now sitting on a large couch, with his head resting on one of his shoulders.

O'Byrne looked over at Ed, "This may develop further and us westerners do not want to be caught up in the middle, so be ready to leave slowly in about ten minutes. And remember that you should never trust anyone, never confide in anyone and be wary of females here in Iraq."

"If I ever come across one, I'll remember."

Chapter 6

The Past and the Present

July 1983–1984.

The recently promoted chief of staff for the MI6 British Secret Intelligence, George Webster, sat silently at his new desk. He had finished re-arranging his new office and now took some time to look from his window at the flowing river Thames below him.

He drummed his fingers on the shiny desk and his mind drifted back over the years. As a young man, he had joined the SIS and now after making the right decisions at the right time had reached a pinnacle in the organisation, and these thoughts made him smile contently. There would be challenges, some new and some that had been with him for some time. He focused on those that were already existing, and those that would still continue to be issues in the near future.

The Troubles with the IRA seemed to drag on over the years. The bombings had continued but Sin Fein, their political wing, was making a name in politics and it was a distinct possibility that a peace treaty might be agreed in the near future. Maggie Thatcher had also started a second term, and this continuation of British leadership might push through a new treaty.

In Iran, the Contra affair, with American hostages held in the American embassy, was at the top of the news and although the hostages were released, the rumour circulated that that George Bush settled for their release at the expense of a huge arms deal, set at $10 million.

The United States department of foreign affairs were also having their problems at this time. In October 1983 they invaded Grenada, and in April that same year, the American Embassy was bombed in Beirut.

Webster lay in wait of the aftermath. He knew there would be new and even bigger challenges during his time that he would need to deal with.

However, there was one area of unfinished business that was most irritating, and for his own peace of mind this would need to be cleared up once and for all, he would need finish what he had started, and it involved tracking down a former IRA member, turned fraudster, called Barney Coughlin.

He was an IRA agent, and although still a novice, specialised in producing and detonating bombs. He was involved in an assassination attempt in the Shetland Islands at an Oil Terminal's opening ceremony. Fortunately, he absconded before the plan was fulfilled, but if he had stayed and was successful, the impact on world affairs would have been catastrophic.

After he left the Shetland there were many who pursued him without success, including Webster's MI6 team, the British Army and the UK constabulary, but none had come close in apprehending him. However, at the time of his new appointment, Webster had identified Coughlin's whereabouts, but the in the uncertainty that followed the attempted attack, Coughlin was able to evade arrest.

Webster was a tall man, and his baldness gave him a clean, superior look, giving him a sense of having the utmost elegance. It was exactly what someone would expect from a British government official, an officer of the realm.

His business with Coughlin had left a bad taste in his mouth and he desperately wanted to close the case, Coughlin was, after all, a person that nearly overstepped the line when he was involved with the assassination attempt of Her Majesty the Queen of England. The audacity of this operation was in conjunction with another, and that was to simultaneously assassinate Pope John Paul II. The overall sponsor of these attacks was the KGB, and it was the Russian's intention to destabilise the Soviet people, in order to distract them from their own problems. The Soviet Union were on the point of revolution and this action was to be carried out to prohibit their fall, and the whole operation was brokered by an IRA man: Michael O'Byrne.

As the months passed, the countdown began, and Coughlin, feeling the pressure, finally cracked. He absconded six months before the planned assassination date.

Both operations went ahead as planned, and while the timing of both was exact, the results were not successful. The attack on the Queen and her party took place but the bomb was placed inadvertently in an air duct, so the resultant blast was nullified and little damage was incurred. Meanwhile, in St Peter's Square, in Rome, John Paul II was shot a number of times but he too survived. It was an attack on the greatest Catholic leader of all time and he survived to see the Soviet Union fall. But the ultimate reward came a few years later, when his beloved Poland was released from the jaws of communism, and the country became free and democratic, largely due to the actions of this great man.

Webster gazed over the river, pondering the situation. Coughlin was small fry, but annoying all the same. He started to drum his fingers.

He had received a report that Coughlin had obtained a second passport and was now calling himself Charles Siddons. The passport holder was a deceased man whose identity had been stolen by Coughlin after the former soldier had served in Ireland and Afghanistan. After retiring, he had suffered post-traumatic stress and had allegedly died whilst swimming in the sea during a holiday. Nearly a year later his wife, Sarah, got entangled with Coughlin.

Coughlin's alias, Siddons, had then moved on and Webster had received reports stating that a man resembling Siddons had been seen in Iraq.

Sitting comfortably in his London office, Webster realised that there were now major problems in the world that would certainly impact British security if he did not act, and the only way he could succeed was to increase his intelligence numbers. So, his first priority in his new position was to recruit.

If he was to be successful in his new role, it would be necessary to put one thing to bed and that was to apprehend this slippery character of an Irishman, even if it meant allocating this as a single task to one of his new operators.

The British government had previously supported the leadership of Saddam, but by the time the Iraq war was in its fourth year, things had changed. His corrupt and aggressive leadership had turned the west against him. The worst of his failings was his horrendous human rights record, and the use of chemical and biological weapons.

The war in the Middle East was Webster's biggest worry, with it being a major threat to world peace. He needed a more intricate intelligence network working within Iraq, a spread of individuals reporting directly back to him.

*****

During a time when Iraq was not doing so well, the Kurds saw their opportunity, and with Iraq committed in the south, they attacked them in the north, splitting the Iraqis defences in two.

With ruthless oppression, Saddam counter-attacked using a concoction of chemical and biological killing, maiming thousands in the process.

Initially Iraq was supported by most European states, many supplying them with anything they wanted, but as the inhumanity transgressed, Saddam's opportunities began to diminish, as their suppliers withdrew their support.

Iraq continued to hold back the Iranians, from the east, and the Kurds, in the North. Saddam was utilising whatever he could to stall the enemy.

Meanwhile, Webster was making plans. He needed to step up his resources in Iraq if he was to keep abreast of the developments and prevent a faraway conflict from developing into a major war.

The more desperate Saddam became, the more dangerous was his behaviour, and Webster wanted to be ahead of the fallout. His intelligence system must ensure that any of Saddam's unpredictable actions would be suppressed before they started.

But the smallest is not always the poorest. The closest and richest country to Iraq was Kuwait, and Saddam was convinced that Kuwait was legally a part of Iraq. This confusion transpired when British surveyors at the end of the Ottoman Empire sectionalised the countries.

Saddam claimed Kuwait was a sovereign part of Iraq and he maintained the British fast-tracked their own claim by hastily reinstating the puppet King Feisal and by doing so, deceived the world.

This situation occurred after the British defeated Germany in 1918. Kuwait was part of the Ottoman Empire, and the tenure then passed to the British, but would later revert to the Arabs when the surveyors set up the boundaries of entitlement.

It is one thing to divide huge areas of land using mathematical theory, but it is another to ignore the rights of moral and tribal heritage, and to divide it by ethical means may have been more appropriate. If this was to be the case it would have benefitted Saddam.

Those countries divided were Iraq, Kuwait, Jordan and parts of Israel, which all subsequently became under the jurisdiction of the victor: Britain.

The boundaries were set into two kingdoms, Jordan and Iraq, and they were presented to the Arab people as a reward for being allies during the war with Germany.

Iraq was then sectioned into three provinces: Mosul, Baghdad and Basra. The British claimed Kuwait as an exception, as its strategic position in the Gulf made it of double importance. Therefore, the British drew up a treaty regarding ownership, but it was one that Iraq did not agree to and claimed it was never endorsed in a court of law.

Webster received his own intelligence regarding a deal between Iran and Israel, with the latter providing Iran with $200 million of business and further deals on the table, this was in exchange for oil.

A variety of weapons were available on the open market and companies based in Europe were still endeavouring to supply Iraq.

Intelligence agencies were aware that should Iraq develop a nuclear warhead, they could be used on the heads of the latest scud missiles. It was generally thought that Iraq was still four years away from this situation.

Chapter 7

One Clever Woman

1978–1983

Demonstrations by students in universities around the globe are normal, young people hungry to put the wrongs of the world to right, they want a voice but no one listens. They feel that politicians and world leaders that gather at global summits talk a lot but do nothing, and feel those involved are old and out of touch. The young need to live in a democratic world and it is understandable that when controlled by dissident leaders, they want change. So, they march in unison, to take a message to their leaders!

But demonstrations are only as good as the publicity they generate, walking around with a few billboards counts for nothing unless the world sees it. It is the media who want sensationalism, and this only comes when police, helicopters, and violence is involved. Protesting is the means by which the youth can try to connect with the world.

Some are arrested, then released, but their antics are stored in the media's memory, it is only then that it becomes a part of history.

Student rallies are limited to countries that tolerate them and are strictly forbidden in others that do not. In these countries without free speech, without true democracy, marching for principles will only result in, prison, hurt and ultimately death.

Political activists reject the censorship of free speech, but the peaceful rallies often, if not always, result in turmoil, and the legitimate demonstrators are then forgotten. In countries where free speech is not allowed, it is more difficult for those who do not want to be violent, who want only to be heard, they are simply arrested.

*****

During the 1980s, the Ba'ath party in Iraq did not allow free speech, and the lucky students who attended good schools and Universities were kept subdued and trained to be subservient. But life was changing, people were more interactive, knowledge was more accessible and education more adaptable. It was the young who were the future, and it was the educated and dissident that was becoming a challenge to any dictator, and this was the case with Saddam.

The Ba'ath party disallowed people to travel freely, even the sick were denied, and this led to the party hiring an Irish medical team of specialists to work within Iraq.

With an intelligent female such as Safiya al Mahdi, the Ba'ath party had a formidable foe, but in challenging them she risked everything she had achieved.

At medical school, she was one of those students that passed everything with the highest marks, always challenging in discussions, and consistently ready to argue her point. She was also a particularly outspoken person with regard politics and human rights.

Her parents were well-to-do Baghdadi residents. Her father had excelled in the world of medicine, but then he took an interest in politics and began following the Ba'ath party, led by Saddam.

It was probably because of his loyalty to the party that Saddam stood by him, especially when his only daughter strayed from his political agenda.

She became a thorn in the side of her family. She threw away the hijab and the traditional Arab clothes, preferring to wear a western style dress, and openly criticised the party her father followed.

The formal educational degrees she earned at university were of the highest calibre, and she earned the right to practice in the city. By not being subjected to practicing within rural Iraq, this allowed her to utilise the best hospitals, and later graduate as a cardiologist when the opportunity came.

After graduating from medical school, she moved through the ranks and soon became a charge ward doctor whilst still in her early thirties. But her intellect soon became her worst enemy, as she had no respect for the police state, knowing that others would then make her decisions for her and she would never allowed her to think for herself. As a result, she became obstinate and politically self-opinionated.

Outside of politics she was popular with both her patients and fellow medical staff, always keeping a professional attitude and willing to give her last penny to those that needed it most.

In private life, as in the hospital, she met her challenges quietly and resolved them methodically, but as time went on, she became more rebellious and objectionable.

Her father died whilst she was still at medical school and the party stood by her mother, providing her with a bursary, while she continued with her studies and maintained a good work ethic.

During her working day, she drew respect from the younger working section of the hospital. It seemed that her individualism rubbed off on them, and when together at social gatherings the group around her could have been from New York or London, as they spoke English fluently and could share views on international affairs.

She met a young foreign student by the name of Jamal Al-Qazi and they shared the same resolute mentality; he was a patient at the hospital and at the time was suffering from a thigh injury that occurred when he clashed with the military at a rally he had organised in the city.

From the time he arrived in Baghdad, his life was suppressed. As a dissident he was arrested on a few occasions, and things only got worse, coming to a head during a day in honour of Saddam Hussein's birthday.

The celebrations were held in Baghdad, which was not a wise move given that it was a critical time in Iraq's political history. The consequences were bloody.

Jamal was injured whilst resisting arrest and taken to hospital. He lay unattended for many hours and the police instructed the medical staff not to attend to him for a while, to let him suffer. He lay with a fractured thigh for over four hours. Later, after being admitted, he was not expected to survive his wounds as an infection developed. He was a foreigner, native of Lebanon, an agitator and an enemy of the state, he had no future in Iraq.

He did have one ally though: Safiya. She found a kindred spirit in his righteous mentality, and she liked him for what he had dared to do in the face of adversity. However, he had paid the price. His health worsened as the infection set in and he needed more expensive medication than what the authorities were willing to offer him.

Luckily for Jamal he was in good hands and Safiya persisted. Her professional care and attention increased his chances, and after six weeks he turned a corner and was expected to survive. The party transferred him to prison to await trial, and as a dissident in a foreign country, his life was now out of her hands.

During his time in hospital, they developed a romantic relationship. She had never met a person who was willing to give up their life for their political beliefs and she admired him immensely.

Then, one evening before his transfer, they talked late into the night and decided that if he was to survive in Iraq, they would need to be married. This would make him an Iraqi citizen and provide him with better medical opportunities. Of course, her traditional Arab family were aghast at the couple's intentions and strongly opposed the marriage.

There was also one important Ba'ath party rule that was to be a major hurdle in their future. It read:

'*In the case of a marriage between an Iraqi and a non-Iraqi, the latter will pay back to the government all costs associated with said* Iraqis *education.*'

He was the son of a modest Lebanese family, it was unlikely they could raise the funds to cover such a hefty bill, but the couple did not care and went ahead with the wedding that was attended by a few medical friends of Safiya.

After the wedding, her family distanced themselves from the couple, and while Safiya felt abandoned, she remained resolute and continued her studies, always hiding the hurt. They had been a very close but sometimes in traditional Arabic families, honour becomes before love.

The couple found accommodation in the medical centre and life was good at the beginning, but as the months passed it was obvious that they would not make a success of it, there were too many differences unforeseen when they met.

Their lifestyles differed too greatly. She did not drink alcohol and her spare time taken with studying for her doctorate, while he was suspended from studying for his Economics degree due to a lack of funds.

Then the situation fell to its lowest level, when his case came to court and he was jailed for two years for offenses against the state.

It was not long before the leaders of the party called for her. She was an invaluable individual that would be an asset in the future, but one that nevertheless would need to be curtailed. They needed to be sure that she knew they were, and always would be, in control.

It was her last year of hospital training, and soon she would be utilised in a formal role in a hospital somewhere in Iraq.

She had immense confidence in herself, and her overall standard both at university and in hospital training was second to none.

Her seniors at the medical institute called her into a hearing and instructed her to apologise to her family, her seniors at the hospital and to the Ba'ath party, who were providing her with these privileged opportunities.

She left the meeting enraged, her usually angelic face was distorted by a scowl, but she had relented and done what they had asked.

For a person of Safiya's character, apologising for having done right was against her principles, but she knew this needed to be done and it did not diminish the fire within her. Because of this oppressive state, she wanted to immigrate but under the current laws of her country, it was forbidden to even travel let alone move to another country.

    In the meantime, her husband fell ill and sepsis set into his leg. He would not live much longer.

Chapter 8

A Need to Know

1983–1985

George Webster had climbed another rung in the ladder and was slowly ascending the SIS hierarchy. Now that he was concentrating on a wider field of intelligence, he needed to expand his team with a wider spectrum of multi-speaking agents.

He was acutely worried that Saddam had already procured a wide range of WMD (Weapons of Mass Destruction) and was stockpiling them somewhere in the country.

It was apparent that none of the intelligence agencies, including Mossad, had discovered where Iraq's storage facilities were located. He needed to step up his own foreign services, in order to get the detailed information he required.

Webster was also interested in a report received from the CIA, implying Iraq had procured nuclear material from Africa. It went on to say that an Italian firm based in the United States had brokered a deal for this material to be purchased from Niger, and shipped to Iraq secretly.

The last section explained how the Italian Mafia, when working under a pseudonym, were carrying out the procurement and shipping.

Webster knew that the Israelis had a better chance of discovering the details before him. Their intelligence organisation was very effective and they were working with people in the same ethnic conditions as the Arab contingent.

The United Nations' weapons inspectors were also busy trying to do the same by identifying the WMD that were in question. This would be an easy task for weapons recorded in the international nuclear register, but not for those that were stored in secret.

He grimaced at this thought, it was absolutely imperative that he should know more, and it was essential that he step up his game plan. He must find and recruit the charming, multillingual, deceitful, and tough persona he had in mind.

The problem with recruiting from a foreign source is taken at risk as those involved can at any time revert to other organisations, and they turn their hand working as a double agent. Without scruples an agent can double their pay for doing the same job, this is very tempting for any ambitious person that has been dragged from the street.

His initial action was to continue to keep in touch with the movements of Coughlin, but not to apprehend him if found, as he might prove to be an asset.

Earlier, he had sent his agent, a man called Bill Gleed to Zambia to investigate what had happened after the police fiasco that led the fugitive to escape and slip through the net. The agent was briefed by Webster and told not to contact him unless he had made significant progress, this whole episode regarding Coughlin was becoming tiresome and he wanted it closed!

Gleed was a dour individual that had seen active duty in Belfast and Malaya. He was a tall, rangy man, full of fun, yet unconventional and non-commutative but had been especially successful over the years and always loyal to Webster. Webster thought if any of his new team were to get close to Coughlin, it would be Gleed, however time was not on his side, as he was due for retirement.

Webster rang the interconnection buzzer for his secretary, "Mary, please come into my office, I need to send a memo urgently. Oh! By the way, I need a list of those agents now on 'unspecific' campaigns." He paused before continuing, "Also, please arrange for Gleed to travel to Baghdad after he finishes his work in Zambia. I need him to find out what is going on with the expats over there, it seems they're running their own bloody secret society."

London, September 1983.

Tom Patten arrived in his office in Paddington early on Monday morning. He had spent the weekend partying at his friend's farm in Hertfordshire, and now it was time to concentrate on a contract to be carried out in Iraq.

The company that he worked for was a large support contractor for the oil and gas industry, and it had secured a turnkey contract with Iraq that involved the design and procurement of a new pipeline and compressor stations. The work was carried out by the Iraqi Petroleum institute and would deliver oil for export from Basra to Turkey. This was one of Saddam's initiatives to improve his oil revenue and it was Patten's intention to be in Iraq when this phase of the project kicked off.

He buzzed his secretary, "Please confirm my flight tickets are ready, and check that the two construction superintendents have arrived in Baghdad, they should be on their way to Basra by now." His thoughts turned to the two construction men who were both experienced engineers, but were also not so young, and with the site so close to hostilities it may turn out to be too much for them.

He thought of the accommodation and began to wonder if the quality of the 'guest house' was up to a reasonable standard. Was the food suitable? Had the Iraqi project leaders assessed the situation?

He checked the two names, Smith and Parsley, then ran his eyes over their history. It seemed that the senior of the two, Derrick Smith, had worked in Iraq during the reign of King Feisal, whilst the other, Ted Parsley, had spent the last few years in Africa. Reading this gave Patten some comfort, knowing that they had already been exposed to some of the harsh realities of this world.

He typed his itinerary on a blank piece of paper and sent it to his secretary Iona, she would process it and send it to the appropriate people.

Patten informed Iona that his business with Edward Copping could be completed on Monday evening at the hotel, but Copping will not travel to Basra on Wednesday, he will stay in Baghdad and obtain a medical certificate registration and work Permit. This is all linked with him satisfying his terms of the contract.

"By the way, Mr Patten, how will you travel to Basra?" asked Iona. She was originally from Sri Lanka but moved to London when she married. She was a caring secretary and very efficient at her job.

"The Iraqis have leased a car for our use, so I will travel to Basra on Wednesday and stay over the weekend and I would appreciate it if you could be available at this time, just in case I need help. And don't worry, you'll be reimbursed should you have to work out of hours."

"That's not a problem," answered Iona, "please ring me anytime, for anything you may need. Oh, and by the way, Mr Patten, I am to understand that one of the two routes from Baghdad to Basra is at the moment extremely dangerous, the road is within range of Iranian artillery."

"Yes, I do understand this is the case, so I'll be sure to take the safer route."

Iona continued, "It's a pity Mr Patten, I did research into the area that you're travelling to and it is has such an interesting history."

"Well, apparently it's the birthplace of civilisation and near to the 'Garden of Eden.'"

"Yes sir, the nearest you will get to it in this area is when you pass a place call called Al Qurna, unfortunately it is now a frequent battle ground, but has periods when it is seems peaceful. It may be a place to visit, as it's says in the Old Testament that Abraham prayed under 'The Tree of Knowledge' and this tree, allegedly, still exists after nearly three thousand years, although I have my doubts. I have read it is almost skeletal… so perhaps it would be best if you take the safer route."

She went on, "How long does the trip to Basra take by car?"

"About six hours, depending on troop movements," Patten answered and smiled, hoping that the conversation had now ended, he just had too much on his mind. Iona took the hint and gathered up her papers in silence.

"And don't forget, Iona, please advise Mr Copping that I will need a meeting with him over dinner on Monday evening. Ask him to book a table for eight o'clock, there will only be two of us, and I will meet him in the bar at seven, we can talk then." He paused. "Oh, and another thing, I will leave early today so please collect my tickets immediately from our travel department and thank you."

"You're welcome, Mr Patton, have a good trip."

Tuesday 19:00 hrs.

Patten left his hotel room and took the lift to the ground floor of the Meridian hotel, where he made his way to the bar. Only two people were present, so he approached the man he thought was Copping, "Edward Copping, I presume." Copping spun around and formally introduced him-self, then turned to his friend and introduced JP.

"Well, I must say, it looks like more of a holiday atmosphere than a country at war." Patten smiled at the two of them.

JP tapped his cigarette into the ashtray and without looking up said, "Before Copping arrived, we were always trying to ascertain when the next scud missile was expected to hit the city, but then along came our friend here and put some logic into the thought. He has worked out a theory of where and when they will strike, and so far, he's been fairly accurate. He says there won't be any tonight."

"Have you, Copping?" Patten hummed, as if he hadn't already heard the story.

"Well, it's still early days. Nevertheless, I have worked out a plan based on certain assumptions, but there is no guarantee, it's just my stab at it and there are many unknowns and only a few givens. It's really no more than a wild guess and I certainly don't want to be responsible for any fatalities."

"I would say you have cleverly tabled an educated guess and that's why we're sitting here tonight!" JP smiled and looked at his new friend fondly.

"OK," snapped Patten, "as we're talking about this very subject, I might tell you that MI6 have been in contact and instructed me to hand over all documents on the subject of scuds. I would stress that if you do not comply, it will lead to a more serious situation with the security services. "

There was an uncomfortable silence. Copping felt invaded, the instruction from his new boss was untimely and too direct, he felt that Patten should not have been instructed by MI6 to do their dirty work, especially in front of a friend.

"That's fine, Mr Patten, I will surrender everything to you tomorrow, and cease any further work."

Patten waved his hand as if it didn't matter, and raised his glass, "To life!" the others repeated unenthusiastically, "To life."

JP, always so dapper and tranquil, now seemed agitated and uncomfortable. He drank to the toast, then picked up his book, stood up stiffly from his chair and excused himself from the company.

Over dinner, Patten approached the subject again and asked Copping how he had developed his assumptions, and Copping explained the situation.

"Have you a formula? Norms? Plans?" asked Tom.

Copping nodded, "And a map with different projections in 'what if' situations."

"In that case, you will need to surrender these as well and then we can close this incident."

Chapter 9

Medical check up!

October 1983

Whilst Patten was travelling to Basra, Copping took a taxi to the hospital designated by the Petroleum Institute, which was located across town. The purpose was to arrive early before the multitudes of people, as it would give him the opportunity to get away quickly. He expected the whole activity would not be more than half an hour.

As the taxi dodged between cars to the hospital, the driver remained calm and was unperturbed by how close he was to other cars. The fear in Copping became intense each time the driver turned his body at ninety degrees to talk to him with a mixture of Arabic and English, as he had the habit of waiting for a reply whilst still in the inverted position, and at the last minute turning back to the wheel, swerving his car wildly as he averted oncoming traffic. On one occasion, the driver held his position for a second too long, and if it wasn't for Copping crying out to him, it could have been complete disaster. Copping was sure it was more by luck than judgement that they all did not end up in hospital.

After about half an hour, the car skidded to a stop outside the hospital entrance and the driver flashed his dirty brown teeth as he smiled upon receiving his fare.

When Copping reached the information desk, it was pandemonium. A crowd of people swarmed the reception, all shouting at the two clerks, each one of them was holding a medical requisition, demanding to be assisted.

The two receptionists appeared perplexed but remained calm, taking one paper at a time and ignoring the demands from others that were waiting.

Copping got into the melee and somehow wormed his way to the front. It seemed he was invisible, perhaps because he was the only foreigner in the room. He tried to catch the attention of the male receptionist with unwavering eye contact, it was the only way anyone could be noticed over the din.

The receptionist appeared to be dealing with those in the reception area, whilst his co-worker sat at the desk and shuffled the paperwork. It was Ed's assumption that she was female, although she wore an ankle length black abaya and a Niqab that covered head and face, so by way of appearance he could not be sure. Instead, he deduced her gender by the higher pitched voice and the slender and graceful movements.

After what seemed like an eternity, the male behind the counter turned to him and shouted something in Arabic.

Copping thrust the form that he had completed back in his office into the man's hand, not knowing what he had said. The clerk looked tired and in a very guttural tongue shouted something while waving his hand in a particular direction, Copping could only assume that he should follow the man's hand.

Copping tried to confirm this by asking again in English and the man replied, saying a word that Copping had construed as 'Outpatients', and pointed in the same direction. So, taking the clerk's advice, Copping followed his vague directions. He then pursued a path that ran alongside the hospital wall, passing a few medical staff, all of whom seemed to be carrying the world on their shoulders, with their eyes fixed on the ground as they passed.

He soon reached the next building, but the sign was written in Arabic and he could not decipher it. He felt helpless, and loitered for a few minutes, waiting for a suitable person whom he felt he could approach and ask the way to outpatient care. However, whenever he approached anyone to ask the way, he was ignored, and they would speed up as they passed him in silence.

He did not get any help and was at a loss in which direction the outpatients department was situated. He continued sauntering along the path and just as he was about to walk under the doorway that led back into the hospital, his eyes were distracted. Quickly glancing to his right, he noticed a woman sitting on a bench nearby, wearing a white coat with a stethoscope draped around her neck. She noticed him hovering and smiled, and when returning her smile, he took a longer look at her. Her face was angelic, with large dark eyes that held his stare just for a few seconds, before she looked down, embarrassed by his gaze. He moved towards her, side-stepping some people coming in the opposite direction and almost tripped as a consequence. They both laughed, appreciating his awkwardness, and his desperation to talk with someone who might help. He braced himself and opened his mouth to speak, but she sensed his difficulties and in a soft, quiet, heavily accented voice asked, "Can I help? Because you seem to be lost." Her face was radiant as she smiled, and the serenity of her face never changed.

Copping felt uncomfortable. This young, beautiful medic, who obviously had an incredibly intelligent mind, was also so graceful, so feminine. Under the midday sun it was difficult, and he had to squint to look more closely, but he soon become accustomed to the brightness and immediately his eyes locked onto hers. For a second or two he was transfixed, but then it was his turn to look away, feeling uncomfortable again.

She stood up and he noticed that she was much shorter than his 1.8 metres. Her physique was full, but he could see under her white overall that she was shapely. She tilted her head slightly as she looked up at him, and he noticed how defined her facial features were, especially her stereotypically Arab nose, which had the slight suggestion of a hook. Nevertheless, it took nothing away from her refined features, if anything it added to them. As she began to speak, Copping noticed her eyes seemed to naturally angle upwards from the nose, in a beautiful almond shape.

"My name is Safiya al-Mahdi and I work at this hospital." She continued, "Normally I am a house doctor on one of the wards, but today I am standing in for a colleague." She paused. "I am looking after outpatients in the A&E ward, but now is my break time, so how can I help you, sir?"

She smiled, her wide mouth turning upwards at the edges. Attempting a more formal introduction, she offered her hand, but as she did so, the stethoscope slipped from her neck and in an unhurried and graceful movement she caught and adjusted it in a single motion. Unlike Copping, she handled herself with style.

When Copping didn't immediately reply, she looked at him and repeated her offer of help.

"You speak English, I presume? And you are looking for something?" Her smile continued, unrelenting.

"Eh, yes, Doctor," he started to put words together but was he was struck dumb.

"Is that the procedure pre-requisite?" She asked and took the form from his hand and quickly scanned it to find out what was needed.

"Oh yes," she continued "You want an X-ray and a blood test with a basic medical examination, so if you would like I can show you where to go."

"Oh no, please just tell me where to go, I really don't want to waste your time."

"If I do not take you, you may never get it done today, because we are told not to talk or mix with foreigners and if we do, we could be accused of being a spy. After all, the country is at war."

"But please, I don't want you to get into trouble," Copping stammered.

She stood up holding the paper and, looking up to him, said with authority, "Follow me," adding, "and don't worry, that is the least of my problems," and she glided along the corridor into radiology department. She then spoke with the attendant and came back to where Copping stood.

"Please sit down, she will call you when she's ready. In the meantime, I will wait outside for you."

Twenty minutes later, he was walking across an open area on the inner part of the hospital, with Safiya walking slowly next to him. "It is another department for the blood test and examination, and once I confirm your appointment with the doctor, I must leave as my break time is up."

"I can only thank you," he replied.

"How long are you here in Iraq for?"

"One to two years I think."

"And your name?" She looked up at him.

"Oh, my name is Edward Copping."

"Where do you stay?" she asked.

Ed was taken aback by her forthright questions, but happy to answer them.

"I'm staying at the Meridian Hotel."

"Will you be based there for the whole of your stay in Iraq or will you go into a house later during your tour here?"

"If I can afford to stay in the hotel, I will try and move over to the Sheraton opposite."

"Why?" she asked.

"It's better over there, especially for a longer stay."

"I hope, Mr Copping, that your medical turns out well for you, and I hope that you enjoy your stay here in Iraq, but I must say goodbye and get back to my duties."

Copping was again lost for words, he did not want her to go and almost choked as he tried to offer his thanks, and nothing came out.

In a few moments, she had gone, and he thought he was in a dream. How could this have happened to him, she just walked out of his life as quickly as she had come into it.

Eventually, a nurse came into the room and called him in, and he sat down on a chair while the nurse strapped his arm, before withdrawing the blood. He thought that his blood pressure would be sky high after meeting Safiya, and that proved to be the case. The nurse had to take it three times in order to get a reading that was acceptable.

She remained silent as she guided Copping to another room where she asked him to remove his shirt, and he positioned himself for the chest X-ray.

"OK, you are clear to go," the nurse spoke in good English, and quickly gesticulated him towards the exit.

Outside in the corridor, Safiya was unexpectedly waiting. She had returned from her duties and was examining a report that she then gave to an orderly standing by.

She looked up. "Hello again, Mr Copping, I will walk you to the door."

"Safiya, thank you for coming back and for all of your help."

"Thank *you,* Mr Copping. Most doctors train and take their examinations in English, but I still have to think before I speak." And with that, her face crinkled up in an elfish smile.

Chapter 10

Iraqi Revolutionary Council

1979–1984.

During the Iraq-Iran war, Hussein and his revolutionary council met regularly. Although, these meeting were carried out without an agenda, it was his method of imposing a fear on his Army officers. He would have already made any military decisions himself outside of this meeting.

Sometimes he would call it to sort out a misconduct or to impose some sort of order on his men, threatening them with death if it was not carried out to his precise instructions.

Any problems that needed to be resolved were unilateral, as with any dictatorship, there is nothing egalitarian about it.

During Saddam's reign he had built many palaces and private dwellings, mainly in discreet areas where the enemy could not easily detect them.

Because of his tyranny, the world around him was directed by security, starting from his Command council members, who were all Sunni Muslims and all born and bred in Saddam's hometown.

Some members were selected because of their technical abilities, although they were never part of the inner circle, only by invitation would they attend.

From every avenue of his regime, Saddam demanded loyalty, politically and domestically, and demanded total allegiance. Without this, there would be no future.

On a day in July 1979 a sinister coup occurred instigated by Saddam Hussein, it was a day when he chose to act as Prime Minister, situating himself in the Republican Palace that overlooked the River Tigris in Baghdad.

Some of the command meetings were digitally recorded and made accessible to the media. However, despite the fact that each recording is carefully edited before being released to the public, this one was not.

During these council meetings, it was not a policy to invite the academics, although sometimes it was necessary to hear what they had to say first-hand, rather than hear it in a distorted report later.

Meetings were dominated by Saddam, and those in attendance never made eye contact with him unless he needed an answer, and if the meeting was to be recorded then a lot of what was said was for the press. The attendees were carefully schooled to understand and appropriately laugh at Saddam's jokes.

Those invited to the meeting were always incredibly conscientious of their interactions with Saddam. This was primarily due to an incident that occurred four years earlier, that brought the utmost fear to all members of his inner circle and set the tone for future assemblies.

Ahmed Hassan al-Bakr was at this time President of Iraq, and though he did not know then, his days were numbered. Saddam, who was his vice president, was planning a coup. But while Saddam had a strong following, he found out that several members of his own inner circle were conspiring to counter this move.

He then ordered the arrest of al-Bakr under some trumped up charge and later, under torture, al-Bakr disclosed the members who were against Saddam. He revealed that twenty-two of the sixty-eight members of Saddam's inner circle secretly opposed him.

Saddam did not waste time and assembled the inner circle. The names of the twenty-two members that al-Bakr had disclosed were called out, and each man that stepped forward was immediately arrested and corralled into the annex room, whilst Saddam addressed those remaining.

He thanked the remaining forty-six members for their loyalty, then abruptly ordered them to go outside, select their weapons from the rack and use them to kill the twenty-two traitors.

Saddam's control of Iraq was beset with inhumanity and cruelty, and there were others at his disposal who were even more ruthless. His deputy, Izzat Ibrahim al-Douri, was extremely clever but also dangerous and psychopathic. His reputation so proceeded him that he would kill anyone that stared at him.

*****

October 1983

Two weeks after seeing Safiya, Copping kept his word and moved across the road from the Meridian to the Sheraton. The deal with the Sheraton gave him a superior double room with a separate lounge, he felt it was a touch of luxury, and in times like this he tended to stay in his room more often. One evening, shortly after the move he came down from his room and was heading into the bar when he noticed that the piano player, a Christian man called Samos, was missing more keys than usual. Copping knew that something must be troubling him, this always happened when he did this.

Samos looked down at his notes and at first ignored Copping, but then without looking at Ed blurted out, "Mr Ed, please go away and do not speak one word. "Al-Douri and his sidekicks are at the bar and if he finds out his piano player is a Christian, he will make trouble for me."

Copping looked at the ground and sauntered away, avoiding the bar and slowly walking out the door. Once he was outside, he dropped his pencil on the floor and as he picked it up, glanced quickly backwards where there were some six or seven men, all dressed in Army uniform. In the split second he looked, he picked out Al-Douri, he recognised him by his reddish hair. Luckily, he was looking in the adjacent direction and that was enough for Copping, who made for the road and hailed a taxi, he would spend the evening across the river. Copping never saw Al-Douri again, and was the only member of Saddam's inner circle that was never caught an sent for trial, although it was reported he was to have been killed in an airstrike, this was never substantiated.

*****

Syria did not have a good relationship with Iraq, and they closed the Iraqi oil export that was routed through their country to the Mediterranean. This had a major impact on Iraq, and their export statistics then fell from over 3 million bpd to just 0.5 bpd. The only means left available for Iraq was to export by truck, a laborious and costly endeavour.

Saddam wanted more pipelines, and the nearest to completion at this time was the southern export facilities, so he ordered his command council to ensure the Petroleum Institute delivered early. This was a direct ultimatum on Mahmoud by the council, a dangerous position to be in.

Mahmoud was fully aware of the consequences if he failed in the time allocated to him, but to achieve this he needed a reliable man to push the productivity and report the slightest deviation to the schedule quickly.

He wanted a reliable person, a non-Iraqi, and one who could report to him honestly and accurately on a weekly basis. This person would have the ability to make the appropriate recommendations to ensure the project would meet the completion dates set by the command council.

The reason for a non-Iraqi was the necessity to speak the truth, and not simply hide behind something that they knew Mahmoud would want to hear. He needed to know what was wrong, not the "everything is fine, we can handle it" approach that he had been told so many times.

He pondered over the situation for many hours, staring at the desert plains, contemplating the task ahead of him. It seemed there were not many whom he could trust, but there was one person, one non-Iraqi, that he was prepared to trust. Edward Copping.

If the availability of these pipelines went according to plan, it could raise the production and export to over two million barrels per day, and the man he had in mind would need that kind of carrot dangled in front of him.

Saddam made his wishes clear to the command council and it would be Mahmoud's duty to reciprocate and deliver what he envisioned. Saddam then ordered a letter be written and waited for Mr Rahim, the oil minister, to draft it whilst at the meeting.

Dear Mahmoud,

You are accountable to me regarding the completion of the pipelines specified in the attachment.

The original dates have been updated to indicate that the first project will be ready for export in twenty-four and not the thirty months originally planned. This will include the completion certificate with all relevant certification.

Signed,
A Rahim

Saddam waited for the letter to be written somewhat patiently, but Rahim's face was white as he received it.

"Thank you, Mr Rahim. And remember, at our next meeting you will report the status."

The meeting finished and Rahim left the room, immediately making a call to his second-in-command, a Mr Aziz.

Chapter 11

A Democratic Ireland

1977–1988.

Seven years had passed since Barney Coughlin had changed his life from being an ordinary Irish village boy, to a trained assassin for the IRA.

It wasn't a decision he made independently; but agreed with his best friend Declan. It is one thing thinking for oneself in normal life, but this changes dramatically when you become a member of a secret military group such as the IRA.

It was a particularly difficult decision for both of them. Their lives were good. They lived in a picturesque village, the beautiful redwood trees that stood proud and straight went down to the loch. There were lush green fields, pubs frequented by friends, and everyone in the village knew each another.

They were both popular in the workplace and in the village, but one thing was missing, it was that all of their close friends had moved away from the village due to the Troubles, and only himself and Declan remained.

Having been left behind, they both wanted to do something for their country, they had heard all the reasons from the elders in the village of the bad times, and the treatment received from the British leaders, so both decided to do something about it. They worked on a plan on how to approach the provisional army and swear allegiance to the cause. They both knew that once this was done, there would be no return.

Then, on a foggy day in the autumn of 1978, they were sworn in to the Irish Provisional Army, and their immediate future was decided for them.

The next twelve months was to be a busy period, with their time taken up by training and inductions. Meanwhile, it was going to be the worst period of atrocities ever seen during the conflict with the British.

This period was also dark for Coughlin. After nearly a year, he could not cope with the violence, the ferocity, and killing of innocent people in the war. He slipped into a depression and by the end of the summer of 1980, he made his move and booked his flights and left the Shetland Islands. He first went to Glasgow, and later moved onto London, where he became just a faceless Irishman, lost in the crowds! He was always conscious that many would be on his tail.

Declan stayed on in the Shetland Islands working on an Oil terminal site, and continued with his work with the IRA, concentrating on the assassination planned for May 1981.

Two months after Coughlin had left Shetland, another partner called Billy, an expert bomb-maker from Belfast, joined Declan.

Coughlin continued to hide and looked for ways to travel somewhere no one would find him. He hid for six months in the south east of England, and later moved to London, where he was lucky to be saved him from a beating on the streets, by a caring lady. Her name was Sarah Siddons a widow, and she put her reputation on the line by taking in Coughlin and nursing him back to health.

He later deceived her and stole her late husband's identity, which provided him with an alias. He then made his way to Africa with his new identity, and started a whole new life under the name of Charles Siddons.

He was initially stopped at the border control, and was danger of being sent back to his previous destination, but was saved from what could have been a dangerous situation by a mysterious African man, called George Mwanza.

After settling in Zambia, he survived undetected there for over two years, under his new alias, and wanted to stay in Africa forever, but his cover was blown after he helped a mother in distress. It was a gallant gesture in helping find her children but one that decided his fate and he was on the run again.

Again, his Irish luck was on his side when he was fortunately reunited with George Mwanza, who provided him with a new passport and a ticket to Ethiopia. When Coughlin asked why he was so willing to help, Mwanza replied, "I am only paying back a debt to you, Charles."

Coughlin had never spared a thought regarding the loan he had given Mwanza. Coughlin had helped him in the past and Mwanza was the man that saved him when entering, and now again when leaving, the country. The debt was paid.

His original fake documents, including a passport, health documents and bank cards, were assigned to Charles Siddons, and it was only with the help of Mwanza that these were changed to Edward Copping, his new identity.

Edward Copping, who had stood tall moving through the border guards when entering Iraq, had built himself a good life since his arrival and was now settled with a good accommodation and well thought off at the Petroleum Institute.

The short-term prospects with Iraqi national oil were good, as long as the war lasted. But on a darker note, a KGB agent with the unlikely name of O'Byrne, who had made it clear that his freedom would only be maintained if he did what he was told, controlled Coughlin's private life. He did not have an option; O'Byrne was in control.

*****

The one small enclave in the British Empire that had not achieved self-rule was Ireland. Even though it was a wonderful country, known as the emerald isle due to the lush green countryside, with it's the warm people and friendly pubs.

History has supported the fact that the Irish have always been subservient to the British. Over the years, their Aristocracy had bought up the land, and soon more foreigners than indigenous people owned the country.

But the Irish have always been willing to fight for their rights, but the many the revolts were always quashed by the British authorities, the promises were always reneged on by Downing Street.

After the British reformation, Ireland remained a Catholic country, and the British, sent to Ireland many Presbyterians to maintain the 'balance' these were later joined by a migrant protestant population from Scotland, who settled in the North, and the local Catholics were stoutly under British Control.

Jealousy and hatred persevered over the years, and the marches and protests by the Irish always came to nothing, with their protests falling on deaf ears.

1900AD–2000AD

During the twentieth century, the fighting and unrest continued, and the British posted a large army in the north of the country that resulted in the troubles.

Then, when the fighting finally ceased, a peace treaty was signed and coalition was agreed between the unionists and nationalists in 1985.

But commitment to the cause prevailed, and in spite of the peace treaty, some dissidents were not convinced and fighting once again prevailed with multiple killings on both sides.

The British Prime Minister at the time, Margaret Thatcher, remained resolute and her aggressive attitude inflamed matters, with the IRA retaliating with a barrage of assaults.

Numerous attacks occurred in the UK during the nineties, with a few on foreign soil, including one on an army barracks in Germany. There was also an incident between some IRA members and a group of British troops in Gibraltar in which several IRA members were shot, heightening the tension between them. But the worst was still to come.

A massive bomb was detonated at a memorial service. It occurred in Enniskillen, Northern Ireland, killing twelve and injuring seventy others.

This even signalled a time to end the hostility, as both sides were now weary of war. The killings had gotten out of hand, and things needed to change. On the 10th April 1998, the Good Friday agreement was signed and is an event to remember.

But this was not the end. On the 15th August 1998, a break-off group called 'the real IRA' carried out an attack in Omagh, County Tyrone. A 400 lb bomb exploded and killed twenty-nine people and injuring over two hundred.

This would be the last attack to date, and while there would be differences in the years ahead, they will be debated verbally in parliament, rather than by the cruelties of war.

Finally, it was a time to rejoice, as there were significant changes that would create a better world.

Our world is not divided by race, colour, gender or religion.
Our world is divided into wise people and fools,
And fools divide themselves by race, colour, gender and religion.
　　　　　　　　　　　　　　　　　　　　　Nelson Mandela

Chapter 12

Meetings and Progress

October 1983

The headquarters of the Iraqi Petroleum Ministry in Baghdad was a building that did not look ostentatious. It was plain, large and uninviting, when it was expected to be a building that exuded wealth. After all, it did represent the single largest part of Iraq's GDP.

On this particular day, a senior group of managers and engineers were assembled to agree the best way forward in terms of furthering the directive from the command council.

At the top of the table sat Mr Ahmed al-Maliki, with the robust figure of Mr Mahmoud next to him, and the project directors who reported to the two senior men were seated on either side of the table.

It seemed that Mr Mahmoud was the main mouthpiece today. Being a large man with a loud voice, he made the situation abundantly clear to those at the meeting. He read out a message that he had received from the command council via the deputy oil minister, Muhammad Aziz, and advised the eight managers present the revised target date and cost will be achieved without recourse. His mood was threatening and to the point. He finished with the term "heads will fall", such was the importance that a chill went through every man sitting around the table.

Mahmoud finished his rant and the table was silent, he then added in a much quieter tone, "Tom Patten, the London based design project manager for the export pipelines, is expected to arrive the day after tomorrow. You have all already met him, and he will travel to the Basra and visit Az Zubayr, and other relevant sites," turning he added, "he will need clearance, Mr Maliki."

Gentlemen, that is the meeting closed."

Two days later.

Four of the five major contract representatives were summoned to attend the Baghdad office, it was short notice and all but Patton knew of Saddam's new demands. He had already arrived from England and was staying at the Meridian, giving him enough time to be briefed by Maliki, and a few hours to meet and talk with Edward Copping.

Two hours later.

After a few beers and a meal, Patten was comfortable with the new employee, although he thought Copping's lack of experience at this level was a concern.

Patten advised Copping of his terms and conditions, and in return he kept Patten up to speed with his medical and visa application.

Copping on the other hand did not mention his connection with O'Byrne or Safiya.

Chapter 13

Home of MI6

Century House, December 1983

The mood had changed within the SIS management, and in 1984–85 George Webster was on the rise within the SIS hierarchy, now holding the senior position as Head of Special Operations with direct responsibilities to the Director General.

During this time, he gained a seat on the influential Joint Intelligence Committee and his political future was in full flight.

But his egoistical nature was getting the better of him, always looking over his shoulder for the one that got away rather than planning for the future. His newly formed and far-reaching private information network had provided him with the intelligence he wanted, but the one informant that caused him the most concern was Martin Valeron. Webster had good reason to believe this man was double dealing.

What caused Webster equal concern was that Martin Valeron had withheld vital information at a time when Coughlin could have been traced and arrested, if only these facts had been provided sooner.

In December 1983 Gleed returned to London from Zambia, and was expecting to travel to Baghdad shortly, but had decided to take a few days holiday before travelling. This provided the opportunity to attend a friend's birthday drinks at a pub in Paddington.

By coincidence Tom Patten had also being invited through another channel, and soon after they had been introduced. It seemed that the two had a lot in common.

During their conversation, Patten mentioned that he had already met Copping whilst in Baghdad and had subsequently interviewed the Irishman. He explained it was a strange set up with his contract, although Copping was responsible to him professionally, he was responsible to the Petroleum Institute construction manager for his day-to-day activities.

Patten explained there were difficulties of employing personnel from London to work in Baghdad, possibly due to the war.

Gleed was hopeful after his discussions with Patten and sent a fax to Webster advising him of the possible breakthrough. He received an immediate reply from his boss.

"Please forward a full appraisal of your friend Patten. The information should contain business details, home address, etc., and but be sure to include his corporate family tree as we need to speak with his superiors and get permission to approach him."

Webster returned to his hotel room, picked up the telephone and dialled a number. It was only a few seconds before it was answered.

"British Consulate, what can I do for you?"

"Hello, Webster here, SIS special operations."

"Yes, sir!"

"Can you investigate the people applying for visas for the next two weeks who are located in Baghdad?"

"I can sir and I'll fax them to your office later today, is that OK?"

"And your name?" enquired Webster.

"Knight, Terence Knight."

"Thank you, Knight." He put the telephone back on the hook.

Later that evening, after finishing his supper at home, Webster opened the consulate folder and sifted through the names that were recorded as having applied for a visa to fly to Iraq over the next few days.

He needed to confirm who else that may be interested in Patten's visit to Iraq, especially if they were either Irish or Russian.

Arriving at work the following morning Webster had one thing on his mind, so he immediately spoke with his secretary who was already at her desk.

"Mary, please check with Gleed, I want his report, and the telephone number of Patten's senior."

"Certainly, sir."

The fax machine was busy over the next few minutes as Gleed's report was five pages long. He had been busy.

"A Mr Coates is on the line, sir, he is Director of Projects and Patten is one of the managers reporting to him Sir. The CEO's name is Kendal, whom do you want to speak with first?"

"Coates, I will contact Kendal in due course." He waited to be connected.

"Hello Mr Coates, my name is George Webster, Director General of the SIS, responsible for special operations."

"Yes Mr Webster, what can I do for you?"

"Your man Patten, I understand that he is travelling to Baghdad, and I want him to do something whilst he is there. You will appreciate that this needs to be done in complete confidence."

"I think I understand you, Mr Webster, and will make that point clear with him. What else do you want him to do?"

Chapter 14

Tried and Tested

February 1984.

The Hotels Sheraton and Meridian both stood just off the square. The former had the disadvantage of being close to the local mosque and on Fridays the hotel side next to the mosque got the full blast from its minarets.

It was normal procedure for long-term hotel guests to change their hotels, moving to better accommodation, on the same deal they initially paid for. It was all about filling rooms and Copping had secured a good deal, and had moved some six months previously, but did not expect for his room to be next to a minaret, and he suffered by the loudspeakers on a Friday at prayer time.

He had moved into a spacious suite, with two rooms and luxurious furniture, without clearing this with Patten. It was a delicate situation as his Project manager normally stayed in a lesser room when visiting.

Patten found it more convenient to stay in the same hotel as Copping, and so Iona booked him his normal regular sized room in the Sheraton, not knowing that Copping was staying in much better accommodation.

After checking in, he made his way to his room on the fourth floor. It was late and he was tired after a long flight, so he decided to retire early and went directly to his room where he undressed, showered and dived into bed.

At the same time Copping, JP and a small group returned from the Melia hotel on the other side of the Tigris. They had gone to there for a nightcap but the military forecast anticipated a scud attack that evening.

They had left a note for Patten informing him about the missile threat that evening, as Copping believed it was possible that the scud could land close to the hotels.

However, Patten's arrival was earlier than expected, so he did not receive the note and was soon asleep.

At four in the morning, a loud explosion jolted Patten awake. He began to panic, quickly jumped out of bed, located Copping's number, and rang it.

"Hi, Copping, it's me, Tom. What was that bang? Was it a scud?"

"Well, that's a good wakeup call, but no, it was probably a practice of the Ramadan cannon going off. You know, to signal the beginning of fasting, go back to bed and get some sleep."

Patten was nervous and lay awake for some time before he slipped into another deep sleep.

As is normally the case with countries at war, they set up an early warning system. It is basically a radar trap that, if penetrated, would set off alarms in the city. Iraq had a similar system set up outside of Baghdad, but no one had informed Patten.

At about five o'clock the barrier was broken and the noise of the sirens could be heard as far as Tel Aviv. Patten, once again, awoke with a start and was beside himself with panic.

He rang the receptionist, "The siren? What's the procedure?"

The receptionist answered, "The normal procedure, sir, is that you must evacuate to the air raid shelter, situated below reception at the minus one level, and you must use the stairs. But—"

If he had waited just a little longer, she would have told him that it was a false alarm, but instead he slammed the phone down before she could say anything further and dashed for the bunker dressed only in his underwear.

In the meantime, Copping had got out of bed and was enjoying his shower. He then got dressed and took the lift to the ground floor where he met some of the other expatriates, who were all tucking into their breakfasts.

During coffee, JP asked Copping if his boss had arrived, as he was surprised he had not seen him yet.

"I'd forgotten about him. I'll have to go back and see where he is."

Copping phoned Patten's room but there was no reply, so he sat down on the bed and tried to guess where he would be.

Then, quite suddenly, his phone rang.

"Where the fuck are you, Copping? I have been trying to contact you for hours!"

"More importantly, Mr Patten, where are you? The rest of the guys and I have been worried stiff, where have you been?"

Patten lost his temper and raised his voice, "So, they've been worried about me, have they? Well, I thought the bloody hotel was being bombed."

He raged on, "First the noise that woke me at four? What was that all about? then the bloody air raid warning goes off!"

"Look, the first disturbance that you heard was probably a practice run of the Ramadan cannon, it, is for all Muslims to start their fasting for the day and this is due to commence for real in June"

"And then the bloody fire alarm?"

"A bird probably just broke the radar screen."

Copping went on, "What did you do?"

"I did what it says on the back of the door! And that is, if the bloody alarm goes off, you evacuate and use the staircase to get yourself into the shelter in the basement."

"OK, Mr Patten, just calm down and I will meet you in the reception."

"No, we're not doing that. Your first job is to get a key for my room, collect some clothes and bring them down to me here, because when I evacuated, I came here in my underwear."

When Copping reached reception, he was denied a key. The receptionist said it was against rules and that she was the only person authorized to take the key to Patten.

Copping smiled, and thought of Patten in his underwear receiving the key from the receptionist. That, most definitely, is worth waiting for.

Later in his room, Patten turned to Copping, "I suppose you and that pretty receptionist had a good laugh at my expense?"

"On the contrary, we thought you did the right thing in the circumstances, but we won't mention this again."

"OK, I don't need breakfast, let's go to the office and you can show me the set up and what Mr Mahmoud has in mind."

"Shall I book a table for dinner or shall we stay in the hotel?"

"Well, you tell me, Ed. You're the one who advises on the dangers in this Garden of Eden. I'll leave it in your responsible hands. Oh, and invite JP if you want, but invite him to my room and we can have a few drinks before deciding where to go."

Later that day.

Copping never mentioned his future hotel arrangements with the Sheraton's manager to Patten. And he was pleasantly surprised when he arrived at Patten's room that evening for drinks. It was a junior suite, similar but smaller than his, and he felt happier with this situation, things would not be so embarrassing if Patten found out the difference.

JP opened the conversation. "So, are we in danger?" He looked at Copping.

"Actually, I did forecast a possibility tonight, but its range should fall short of us by a mile."

"A mile? So the saying 'miss by a mile' counts for something then?" Patten laughed.

"We'll probably be all right, especially as we are on the downstream side of the missile approach. That's just a bit of information I picked up last night in the bar from the three Mossad agents. But I couldn't confirm anything they were saying because the bar was so bloody noisy, but at school I did study modern Hebrew."

"What time is—" Patten did not have time to finish his query, as there was a tremendous blast that shook the hotel. The window that was left open and the curtains blew high into the room, the windows remained intact, but the room was swirling with dust, paper waste and hot air.

When everything settled there was an eerie silence, and it was only then that Copping and JP noticed Patten lying flat on the floor with his hands over his ears.

"What the f—! This is beyond insanity, and why aren't you two on the floor with me?"

JP chuckled and remained where he was, sitting on his chair smoking his cigarette as if nothing had happened.

"We've had this happen a few times before and there's not a lot you can do once you hear the blast."

Copping slowly raised himself from his seat and went out onto the balcony to look at the road below. "Nothing's been obviously damaged, and I expect the air movement from the blast travelled up a few streets before we felt it."

"And tell me, exactly what was your estimate tonight? Was it correct?" Patten asked, with an air of disbelief.

"I don't know where the explosion occurred, but it seems it wasn't that far off. If you consider the timing as well as the distance, it was certainly in the same ballpark."

"Is that what you think?"

"Possibly."

Patten was trembling, "This is bloody ridiculous, I might have to pull you out of here, Copping."

"Don't jump too fast, Mr Patten, everything's fine."

Chapter 15

Three-Card Trick

Spring/Summer 1984

It was over year since Copping had received his new identity, and so far he had not been questioned about his documents. His life was proceeding without any undue complications, although O'Byrne was a thorn in his side.

Unfortunately, O'Byrne was a ghost of Copping's past. He was his superior in Shetland and at the time was already known to the police. He was arrested at Glasgow airport and sent for trial, but through lack of evidence he was released, and later Copping heard that he had died. Then, out of nowhere, this man suddenly reappeared in Iraq, claiming he was a KGB agent.

*****

Mahmoud was ensuring that Copping was working extensively during business hours, but it was after work that his life really began.

First and foremost, it was O'Byrne who wanted reports, then the tennis reservations needed updating, he also played three times a week, and if he had the time, he would visit the British club and get up to date with the social events.

And last, but not least, he would have a nightcap with JP.

On one occasion, Richard whom he played darts with, introduced him to his sister-in-law, a beautiful Kurdish girl called Leila and it wasn't long before he became fascinated by her. She was tall with a full body, dark flowing hair, dark eyes and a huge smile, like the type of woman he had only seen on screen, like a gypsy queen.

Her sister was married to Copping's darts partner and she was now a UK national. It seemed to Copping that this situation might suit her as well. He was entranced with her charm and welcomed her friendship but thought it would be better if things were kept at a distance, he did not want to stray from Safiya.

By now, Copping had been allocated a car as a business perk from the Petroleum Institute, which would make his life a lot easier. He was spending much of his time at the club and driving saved him an hour of walking, but the main attraction at the club was Leila. He was not experienced with girls, having had probably only three interactions with females in his life so far. But he did not like being reminded of that situation, his deception was not a pleasant memory.

However, Leila was a different matter. He was becoming infatuated by the day, but his attraction was founded more on curiosity rather than anything sexual. She was so different to everyone he had met before. It had become an annoyance that she was always at the club before he arrived and raised his suspicion that she might be there for someone else.

His job was currently going well, although he had not travelled to Basra in recent weeks, mainly because of her, and he knew O'Byrne and Mahmoud would be onto him soon, each for different reasons.

Copping's main issue was that he had too many bosses. Tom Patten was his professional boss and controlled the quality of his work whilst sitting in a desk in London, and Ahmed Mahmoud was his technical boss working in Iraq.

The latter was more aggressive than Patten and this strangely suited Copping, as the Director always followed up on Copping's suggestions and recommendations, not always agreeing with him but always acknowledging his point. He valued the work that Copping had done so far on his behalf and despite Copping already controlling four large sectors of construction; Mahmoud was about to give him further responsibilities of a classified nature. This would make him invaluable, but also dispensable. This classified information put him in danger.

The Iraqi project manager Ahmed al-Maliki was based in an office closer to the city centre and this gave Copping a chance for leaving the hotel later than normal. His office was only a three-minute walk from the hotel, which was a lot easier than the forty-five-minute coach drive to the construction offices.

Meanwhile, outside of work, Copping started to become involved in various sports at the club and this brought him into even closer contact with Leila. It wasn't long before he began picking her up near her home, and they began partnering with each other for darts and snooker matches.

They went for dinner together in a foursome with her sister and brother-in-law, and it was after one of these occasions that Richard informed Copping that if he was to marry Leila, he would need to reimburse the state for the cost of her education. He said it was a form of tax and the amount might not be as high as he would expect. He added, "This may be a thing in the future, but not for now."

Copping was now a concerned man, and how much would he be liable for in the case of Dr Safiyer?

Chapter 16

A Guest House in Az Zubayr

Spring/Summer 1984

The darts and snooker sections of the quadrangular tournament had confirmed teams and the dates were set for the tournament to begin, and everyone involved was looking forward to start especially after the games in 1983 were postponed halfway through the year due air raids on Baghdad

Copping had volunteered and subsequently selected to participate in each of the sections, but this would prove to be a tough task, especially with his private diary being so full. One thing he had neglected was completing his weekly report to O'Byrne, which was the most vital obligation to fulfil, in order to keep his life intact.

Copping was now reporting to Mahmoud on four parts of the construction work associated with Saddam's latest drive to export more oil, and it seemed the command council was putting more emphasis on this aspect.

Mahmoud seemed to have grown older since he was first introduced to Copping. It was clear that the worry of completing the projects was taking its toll. Meanwhile, Copping still had not been briefed on the classified fifth project that he was to manage, which was apparently much bigger than those he currently had under his wing, and was under the strictest veil of secrecy.

For the command council to take such an interest in such small projects made Mahmoud excessively nervous, he was the man in the direct line of fire and under no circumstances did he want the projects to fail. He would do what he had to do, even if it meant taking on a foreigner to achieve such a goal.

Mahmoud never attended project meetings but he was always aware of the detail that was discussed. This was achieved by interviewing each of his managers independently, and his final interview was with Copping.

Copping was held in good esteem, but the managers knew he was in Mahmoud's confidence and this created tension.

*****

The guest house near Az Zubayr had, for some years before the war, been used as a club house for the local golf course. While you might expect from this description that it was a glamorous place to stay, you can be assured that it was not. It was dirty and virtually defunct, except for when used by the army during manoeuvres, it was very close to the military front line.

It was also close to the border with Iran, but Patten knew it was the only realistic accommodation for miles, and he made this clear to the two superintendents at the interview.

Derrick Smith and Ted Parsley had already made the guest house a home and, hardened men as they were, did not complain openly.

The place was far from desirable. The rooms were old, the walls marked and rotting, the lighting dim and the furniture decrepit. But they were both approaching sixty years of age, and had probably seen worse. It was now up to Copping to raise the spirits of the men and get them aligned, and he decided to do this on his next trip to Basra.

The two men settled in quickly, befriending the staff and finding a full-sized snooker table in one of the adjoining buildings. Then, after brushing off the dust and cleaning the snooker room, they also turned one of the other rooms into an acceptable recreational area.

A maid attended to the accommodation daily, dressed from head to foot in a black heavy Nida Abaya. She cleaned relentlessly, always sweeping, polishing and dis-infecting, but it seemed whatever she did made little difference to the grim conditions.

The mornings were the worst, in the winter it was bitterly cold and the shower sprayed water inconsistently out of its blocked nozzles, sometimes freezing cold, then sometimes almost boiling. This change of temperature often happened in a second, and the shock of the sudden change could make the user either slip onto the dirty looking tiles or get scalded in the process.

At breakfast there was no way of knowing how long the buffet food had been sitting there, so it was best to take a black coffee and hope that the waiter had boiled the water and washed the cup.

Both Smith and Parsley opted for the coffee that was served in their mugs, bought from the local outdoor market.

On Copping's initial visits to site, the two older men always joked about the accommodation. They would jest with him that he cuddled up to Iraqi bosses and by doing so got the prime job, while they, the elder statesman, had to suffer at the guest house.

Summer 1984 - Thursday

It was early May in Baghdad and the air was hot. The sun shone through a gap in the curtains and woke Copping from a deep sleep. This morning he felt nauseous, his stomach ached, and it wasn't long before he rushed to the bathroom. He remained sitting inert for some time but later, when he felt brave enough, he ventured downstairs. Though his stomach did not settle for long and he constantly had to rush back to his room for relief. It was difficult for him to leave the hotel, but finally his impatience got the better of him, and he stormed out of the hotel and into the sunlight and fresh air! But in a few minutes the sharp and agonising pains returned and he ran back post haste to his room, on the way dreading that the lift up to his room would not be available when he so desperately needed it.

Once back to safety, he imagined that if the guys in the guest house knew of his condition, they would laugh at him, saying something along the lines of, "He gave himself the best job in the best place, now let him suffer!"

It was his duty to travel to the site, but in his state it was impossible, he would have to cancel until further notice. He stayed around the hotel for a further two days drinking only water, but that too passed through him quickly and he felt he would soon be severely dehydrated.

On the Monday evening some four days since contacting the unpleasantness, he felt that he could wait no longer and decided to persevere and make the journey, even though it was daunting given his circumstances. That evening, he carefully planned his trip, down to the last minute.

His drive south was generally uninterrupted, and he was not held by traffic congestion, nor did he experience any Iranian shells. His detailed planning paid off, and he arrived at the 'guest house' in under five hours, but on arrival immediately rushed to the toilet.

It was now around midday and he made for the restaurant, hoping to catch Smith and Parsley at lunch.

"Well, I never." It was Parsley grinning from ear to ear. "So you made it?" He was really enjoying the situation.

Smith was talking to the waiter, an old and wrinkled little man who was taking his order for breakfast.

Then, he came around to Copping, "Your order, sir?"

"Nothing, thank you. I have an unsettled stomach."

In a mixed dialect, that Copping could barely understand, he heard him say, "You mean you have… the shits?"

"Yes, that sums it up in a nutshell."

"Then you must come with me and I will give you something to take tonight and in the morning, but nothing else no food, you understand."

"Um no, thank you. I will abstain."

"No, sir no, you will come with me now," and he tended to the back of Copping's chair, as if to move him out.

This seemed to persuade him and he followed the waiter obediently. When he entered the kitchen, it smelt of grease, an array of unhygienic-looking food was on display, and the kitchen staff seemed busy, constantly shouting and moving around the kitchen doing their work.

Nothing was said between them, whilst the waiter looked for his ingredients and carefully picked out an onion, he then felt it and quickly peeled the outer skin.

"Sir, you listen, very important." He continued to cut the onion into small pieces.

"You only eat this portion now, it is strong, called a Basra onion," and he handed Copping a small plate. He continued, "You eat remainder before sleep, you understand, no food. Nothing."

"No, really, I am OK, but thank you."

"No sir, no thank me, you do as I say and you be OK in the morning, then you eat my soup and bread."

Copping hesitated at first but finally relented. He ate the first portion with his face screwed up and then bent over and started to wretch."

The old Arab then passed a cup of coffee and said, "You drink now, and you must take the other portion of onion later. I will wrap them up. Remember, no food, no alcohol, you understand?" He walked off mumbling to himself before he received an answer.

Copping took the remaining onion, now wrapped in paper, and pushed into his pocket to eat later.

Thursday morning, 07:00 hrs.

Copping was the first at the breakfast table and a waiter glided up to him.

"Yes sir, what would you like?"

"Is Abdul, who served me last night, working today?"

"No Sir, he will come later, it is me who will take your order."

"Then I will have the fried breakfast."

"Everything?"

"Yes, all that you can serve on one plate." He could not wait to eat his first good meal in a long time.

Summer/Autumn 1984 - Thursday morning, 10:00 hrs.

That morning, Tom Patten arrived. He had stayed overnight in Baghdad, taken a car very early in the morning and had arrived in time for breakfast, impressing the other three that were already seated.

Later, he visited the sites chaperoned by Copping and although this took most of the day, it meant he could return to Baghdad, and then to London, sooner.

After Patten had departed, Smith and Copping walked the sites where the work was to be done. They inspected the construction preparation and used the car to drive to each stage, tracking the route of the pipeline as they did so.

They had already checked out Umm Qasr and Warbah, when Smith advised that they should stop of at Safwan where a Mr Kim, the North Korean site manager, was working. His company had a sub-contract with the Iraqis and he was in the process of preparing the groundwork.

"Come," said Smith, "I will introduce you to Mr Kim, but be careful, he is a very excitable individual."

"I did not know the North Koreans were working here, are they useful?"

"They work hard from the day they arrive and never look up. Then they stay that way until the day that they leave, that is not seeing nor speaking for the whole time they are here."

"Then why is the work behind schedule? If they work as hard as you say." It did not seem to add up.

"Because, they have been transferred to Project 109, which is a priority contract and one that Saddam has special interest in."

"Yes, I have heard, but I am more interested in our own contracts not being late."

Mr R. T. Kim was at his desk typing on his computer and hardly acknowledged Smith and Copping as they entered his office and took a seat.

"Mr Kim, we have come for an update on your progress and to agree on a date when you will vacate the site and allow the civil contractor to start work."

Kim did not look up but he stopped what he was doing, as if he froze.

"What you say?"

Smith was about to reply, when it seemed all hell broke loose.

Kim jumped up and with one sweep of his hand, cleared the desk in front of him, sending all the items in front of them clattering to the floor. He then looked up and glared at the two men on the other side of the desk.

"You want me to do everything on your projects. The Baghdad office want me to do everything on Project 109. I need more men and machines otherwise it is impossible!"

"How much work is there to be done on Project 109?"

"There is plenty! I am a civil engineer, not a mining engineer, and most of that job is underground." He then clamped his mouth shut and pointed to the door. "You go, we finished!"

They both hurried out of his office, feeling that the last thing he wanted was to push him any further. They were intimidated by such an erratic temperament.

Copping thought to himself, *This Project 109 is classified and underground, better that I do not make idle talk with others on this subject.*

They finished the tour and returned to the site office to find a note from Patten, explaining that he had left for Baghdad.

*****

Patten took his flight back to London and was happy with his short visit, as all seemed well with the project. Copping seemed up for the job and, most importantly, Mahmoud liked him.

Chapter 17

Learning a New Language

Autumn/Winter 1984

Copping stayed on site for another week. He had lost the infection or whatever it was in his stomach, and with that over he could catch up with the guys on site and get to know them better.

During this time, he mixed with the local contractors as much as he could, picking up a few Arabic words in the process.

However, with a day left before he had to return to Baghdad, he got embroiled in a misunderstanding with a local mechanical engineer called Ismail, an Iraqi who had graduated from Bristol University in the UK. Their disagreement concerned a particular steel alloy and its relationship to strength conditions.

The misunderstanding was brief and, in a few minutes, both were laughing and slapping each other on the shoulder.

"When do you return to Baghdad, Edward?" Ismail asked.

"In the next few minutes," replied Copping. He wanted to get on the road sooner rather than later.

"It would be great if you can take some documentation back to the office. I want to return a few documents to the archives, you know, the daily log, weekly test certificates…"

"Of course, anytime." Copping smiled, "It's not a problem."

Ismail jumped up and leapt out of the office, returning in five or six minutes carrying a large box that he put down on the floor. Then, turning to Copping, "Here is a present for your troubles."

"Can I open it?" Copping asked.

"Yes, of course. It's only something small."

Copping opened the package carefully and was surprised to find a red and black chequered head-robe and a black round head band.

Ismail said, "When you get back to England this will remind you of my country and, I hope, of me too." In Iraq the cloth is called a Kafiya and the cord is called an Iqal."

"That is a fine gesture, my friend." They shook hands.

Copping was asked to take Derrick Smith, one of the site superintendents, back to Baghdad but as he would not be ready until five in the afternoon, he had a few hours to kill and decided to take some time off and inspect the Shatt-al Arab waterway.

The drive took him an hour, it was a lot longer than he had expected, and when he arrived, he drove along the riverbank and parked the car close to the water's edge.

With hardly a ripple on the surface it was hard to understand the tranquillity he felt in a country at war. How graceful those two dhows were as they moved through the water. The smaller boat had a light cream sail and was going in the opposite direction to the larger boat, it displayed a magnificent deep-brown sail, as the larger one seemed to find it difficult to maintain its speed.

An Iranian light cruiser was moored on the Iranian side and there was little human movement on the boat.

On the bank closest to Copping some fishermen were unloading a batch of small fish, and took no notice of the two Arab men who boarded a small houseboat moored close by. Copping was only a hundred yards away sitting on a bench, dozing.

The salon or living room on the boat was small and there was not adequate space for the new arrivals to sit with the two that were already seated at the table. Yet somehow, they compromised, and one poured some tea that they sipped before talking business.

"This war is affecting our operation. We must find ways to increase our income." One of the men, the first to sit, had opened the conversation.

"Even if our roads are not being bombed or patrolled by idiot policeman, our customers are still too scared to come out for business. They're too nervous to take any chances." The smaller one of the group made his mark.

"Whatever, we must step up our operations. We need more supplies, another vehicle, and more activity in the field."

Ismail, one of the new arrivals, spoke up. "Look, my friends, I have put myself on a limb in setting up a small courier action between Basra and the capital, and it is shielded by a business seal, so we can use this for the next year. It will carry ten kilos maximum, but at least it will keep things moving. The business is growing, and I must be careful how much I take out of the batches when they arrive from the tribesmen. If they find a shortage, it will be dangerous, especially as they each take their share. If they're greedy, it will be noticeable."

"How often does it get uplifted from here?" the small man asked.

"Every week, but it depends on local military action."

"We need a better trade route, my contribution is too small, perhaps we can go through Iran?" Ismail was searching for a reliable alternative to his own contribution through Baghdad.

The fat man squeezed in near the porthole, put his arm on the table, and spoke for the first time. "Our business of raising money for our cause has difficulties when we are in the middle of a war. There are only a few ships moving out of here and our only chance is to deal through Europe, the Eastern bloc, or the States." There was silence and he went on, "Our leader will need to be ready when *we* are ready to strike, so our deals need to be larger and more direct. My suggestion is to deploy trucks that travel from here to Europe and beyond."

Ismail spoke up, "We have trucks at the site travelling back to Europe, most of them are empty, and I could try this route, but the clients must be aware of our account numbers and who will enforce this if they default."

"We have agents in Amsterdam, let us try this route first, and our leader Abeer can make more serious decisions when he meets us."

"Yes. Yes," said the man making their tea, "Abeer will advise us what happens next, so let us meet when we next hear from him."

The senior man finalised discussions, "If there is any news, remember to use only coded messages and we meet then."

They all departed separately with ten-minute intervals. Ismail jumped into the site car and in a cloud of dust drove towards Az Zubayr, passing Copping as he dozed on the bench.

The sudden roar of a revving engine stirred him, he looked up at the car as it passed by and was sure the driver he had seen was Ismail. Even if it wasn't him, it certainly was his site car.

Copping began to wonder whether his friend had permission to be away from site, and whom he had notified of his absence. He knew the rules that required anyone departing from the site to complete a form of absenteeism, including a statement as to why he was leaving, and there were no exceptions.

On the drive back to site to pick up Smith, he could not help but think of the driver of that site car. He was sure it was Ismail.

*****

Autumn/Winter 1984

Before flying back to London, Tom Patten visited the Petroleum offices just outside of Baghdad. He unpacked his car and took a bag of books to the first floor and left them in Sadr's office, then walked down the corridor and entered Magarian's office and shut the door.

"Did you want to see me?" he asked the man behind the desk. He was dressed in a light grey suit and a dark blue tie, and looked up as soon as Patten walked into his office.

"Please sit down, there's a favour I want from you, Tom."

"Of course, if there's anything I can do, then please do not hesitate to ask." Patten was cheerful, he was looking forward to going home.

"I don't know whether you are aware of my situation, but I am Iraqi-born with Armenian heritage. It's a long story that goes back to a time when the Turks persecuted our people, but those that were lucky enough to have survived travelled anywhere to escape the massacre, and my ancestors moved here to Baghdad. For all intents and purposes I am an Iraqi, but the Armenian nation needs to maintain its heritage, so I strongly support the ideal."

"That's what I really admire," said Patten.

"After the persecutions some of those who survived started a movement and established a headquarters in London, and now I would like to communicate with those who run that organisation. So, I was hoping that you would take some letters back to London for me, and I would pay your expenses if you deliver them personally."

"Not a problem, if you can give them to me before I leave, they will be duly delivered."

"Thank you, these are the letters." And he handed Patten a sports-bag that was stuffed tight, and extremely heavy when he picked it up. It was, he thought, around twenty kilos. Later, as he stumbled out of the office carrying the bag, all he could think of was his expense sheet.

Chapter 18

Balancing the War Effort

Autumn/Winter 1984

It was the start of the weekend and a good day at the office, when Sadr entered Copping's office at midday and advised the team it was a military holiday, so they could all go home early and celebrate.

An hour later, Copping was in his room where he went straight to the fridge, opened a beer, slumped into the armchair, and thought about what he was going to do with the rest of the day.

He began to think about the multiple sport tournaments his team had entered for the second year running, they were planned over the next few weeks providing the government does not shut down due to the danger of missiles.

The tournament was due to start in two weeks' time. He felt so comfortable sprawling on his easy chair, mulling over his social schedule, that he wondered whether it was worth leaving his room. However, the tranquillity did not last long, and with a mouth full of beer, the telephone rang. Wearily he lifted himself from the chair and picked up the phone.

"Hello, Copping here."

There was silence for a few moments, and Copping was about to repeat his name when a gentle voice replied, "Hello Edward, this is Safiya."

Copping was suddenly overcome by the sound of her voice.

He tried to put on a happy tone. "Oh, hi Safiya. How nice to hear from you, it seems so long, where have you been?"

She avoided the question. "It's nice to hear your voice too, Edward. What are you doing today?"

"Eh, nothing. I've just got in from the office."

"Can I come and visit you?"

"Of course, shall I meet you in the hotel restaurant?"

"That would be nice, but just coffee and perhaps a cake, yes?"

"That sounds fantastic, let's say in an hour, at two o'clock?"

He heard her giggle. "See you then, Edward."

One hour later.

It was hot, and Copping had a long shower, allowing the cool water to run over his head. He then dried himself, rubbing the towel hard over his body. It was difficult for him to get completely dry due to the heat, so he moved to his bed and lay still. The ceiling fan above him was rotating fast and it took only a few minutes for him to dry.

Looking dapper in a sky-blue shirt and grey flannels, he bounced down the hotel corridor, and bypassing the lift, he hopped down the staircase taking two steps at a time. He planned to get to the restaurant early, in case Safiya was sitting by herself. He knew he did not have the same desire for Leila as he did for Safiya, he thought with Leila it was just pure mystery of her that lured him.

The restaurant 'maître de', his name was Nassim, met him at the door. "Good afternoon, sir. Your party has arrived, they're on table 7."

"Party, Nassim? What party?"

"There are some ladies, very nice ones."

"Thank you Nassim, I will find the table myself."

Passing the columns at the start of the restaurant, he came into sight of the table and froze in surprise. There, smiling in the centre of a band of glorious women, was Safiya, looking completely relaxed. He counted five others, all young ladies, talking and chatting. He had not seen a group of Iraqi ladies dressed like this in Iraq before and it made him nervous.

If some busybody thought he was encouraging them to dress and act like a westerner in a public place, it would not end well for him.

As Copping made his way over, Safiya provided a space for him next to her. She looked radiant. She then held up her hand,

and the others stopped chatting and looked towards her and in turn, she introduced each of the ladies in her party.

She explained they were all medical doctors, qualifying in the same year, though she added not at the same university or the same country. Some, she said, passed their degrees in the United Kingdom, unfortunately not in Ireland, and she laughed at her jest.

Copping turned to Nassim who was wavering in the background.

"Nassim, please ask them all what they would like and charge it to my room."

"Of course, sir." He then busied himself, asking the girls for their orders. The atmosphere seemed positively charged. They were talking work and politics, and the conversation often turned to the subject of war, which only made him tense.

Maisha, a dark and beautiful doctor sat opposite Copping, explained that she studied in Edinburgh. "I miss that life. I experienced so much in Scotland, I was so free and found it comfortable that prejudices rarely existed in those people that I met. Although, I did learn that a great antipathy existed between two football teams called Rangers and Celtic."

"Well, Maisha, now you can understand that intersectional differences exist in all parts of the world, and not many of them are as fierce as Rangers and Celtic." He thought for a moment and carefully selected his words, "In Ireland we have a serious problem between Catholics and Protestants, In the main cities in the UK we still have experience with racial tension, and in the Soviet Union they still have a problem with free speech."

Farida explained that she had studied at Imperial College London. "I didn't get into Oxford, but I had good apartment in Acton which I shared with some great people. We had so many parties, I miss those wonderful times."

Three other doctors who had studied in Iraq introduced themselves. These women were a little more conservative, but they spoke English very well. There was Aisha, Habiba and, of course, Safiya. Habiba spoke for them all, "We studied here in Baghdad, but the star is Safiya. She got a first in everything she did, and that was in two different countries."

"Which two countries did you study in, Safiya?"

She looked up at Copping, "Oh, it was Cairo university, then I did my last two years in Beirut, the American university. That's why I do not speak English as well as Leila and Aisha, I only spoke in English for the final two years of my studies."

*****

It was an exciting lunch for Copping and meeting these girls made his day. It was almost sad to see them each drift off and make their way home.

"Edward, you know the rules in Baghdad. There is no mixing with foreigners, which both I and these ladies do not agree with, and the same goes for most of the laws in this regime." Safiya pulled a face. "But let us be happy now."

"For your own safety, please don't speak like that," Copping warned her.

"I am careless with security I know, but they need me more than I need them, and to be honest, I don't care."

He felt uncomfortable and Safiya was aware of his unease.

"Come, Edward, I must go, but I will see you again, yes?"

"Of course, Safiya, shall we make a date now or will you phone me? Unless I can phone you?"

"Edward, there is a war going on and I never know when I have a day off. So please, I will phone you."

They parted as they reached the foyer. He did not kiss her, but he wished he could.

Three hours later.

Copping made his way back to his room feeling elated. He was not a self-proclaimed ladies' man, he could count the girls he had slept with on one hand. He had just never been able to hold down a relationship for more than a few months, and never felt the urge to get close to someone and make a relationship worth lasting.

With Safiya, it was the first time he felt he wanted the union to last forever. He could not wait until the next time that they met. It was a sound relationship, completely different from the more casual one that he had with Leila.

He was jerked into reality by the ring of the telephone and rushed to lift the receiver, hoping it was Safiya.

"Hello?"

"Is that you, Ed? Richard here, are you still coming down to the club? We have the first of our darts games, it is earlier than planned, nevertheless you are in the four to play."

"I will be down in about an hour, is that OK?"

"It is, but I have Leila here and she is surrounded with admirers. Nevertheless, she's looking forward to seeing you again, so please don't be longer than an hour. We'll just order lunch in the meantime."

"Remind me," enquired Ed, "who are we playing this time?"

"Should be easy, it's the Indian contractors. I don't think that they are any good, but you can't take anything for granted here."

"OK, see you in about an hour."

One hour later.

When he arrived, Leila was playing darts with a guy he was not familiar with. They were playing against Richard and Hana, Leila's sister and brother-in-law. Leila half turned and smiled at Copping as he came in, she looked even more stunning than the last time he had seen her. He now felt guilty that he should be lusting after a female friend when he had done the same a few hours ago with another.

As she threw the darts, he studied her. She was a million miles away from his life back in Ireland, not only because of her culture but because of her exotic appearance. He guessed she was in her late twenties as she carried her voluptuous frame elegantly, always with a straight back, despite her heaving bosom. But it was her lipstick and high, rouged cheekbones accentuated her face that was so outstanding. Her eyes were as black as her hair, their huge almond shape honouring her heritage. She was dressed in a sleeveless red waistcoat, covering a white blouse that was unbuttoned at the neck, so that when she threw a dart the upper part of her breasts were exposed.

She looked fantastic, but the situation seemed bizarre, playing darts in the middle of a Baghdad. This was the second time that he had to remind himself that he was in a Muslim country.

He glanced at her legs, shapely and long, covered with navy blue trousers that went down to her high heels. He wondered if it would be possible to walk along the streets with her in downtown Baghdad, or would he be arrested?

After the game, those playing shook hands and all walked towards the lounge, except for Richard and Leila who joined Copping. The greetings between them were warm.

He was besotted. He made his play and kissed her on both cheeks, holding her a little too long. Richard intervened, "I am off to the lounge, so join us if you so wish."

Leila started the conversation. "I've heard about your talents from Hana and Richard. I'm to understand that you are good at darts and other sports."

"No, I'm only a good trier." Copping was nervous.

However, despite his nerves and thoughts of Safiya, the evening went well and later Copping won his doubles match. And now they were thinking of how they could finish the evening.

One week later.

Richard was informing Copping of the competition results so far, when he made sure to make a point of the fact that Leila was still waiting to be asked out.

"You are looking at a gift horse in the mouth. Oh, and by the way, we have the snooker coming up and then the cricket, so your time is limited."

"I know she is beautiful, and I will ask her," Copping promised.

He then pondered over their conversation. He really wanted to date this beautiful woman, but he was already overwhelmed by her interest in him and wanted to be cautious.

He knew of other westerners that were coerced by beautiful women into marriage. By marrying a European they are able to experience freedom, as they can travel anywhere in the world on a western passport, and are finally able to have a sense of security. Perhaps he was being presumptuous. *Stop overthinking,* he thought, *just be positive and enjoy her company.*

So, he phoned her and arranged a date, and made a point of ordering a taxi to pick her up so that they could have dinner at the hotel.

*****

Copping drove to the British club, he wanted to find out information regarding the upcoming cricket match. It was particularly interesting because the first match would be against the Irish medical group and the winner would go on to play the Indian catering group, probably the best of the four teams.

The Indian group also drafted in cricketers who had no obvious connection with them, these players only wanted to participate for the fun and the social aspect.

One man called Wally Wright had agreed to play for the Indian team, and he was particularly interesting because he was alleged to have played cricket for Sussex and might be a match winner for the them.

One particular point of interest, was already well known within the expatriate community, was his likeness to Ed Copping.

Copping checked the draw on the notice board and realised he could face Wright in the final, but only if both teams were successful in the semi-finals. The first matches would be played over the next two weeks, and the final would be soon after, with all of the matches taking place on Friday's, the Muslim weekend. Copping was quite excited about the tournament, and with a spring in step, he returned to the hotel.

The following Friday.

In the final of the cricket, the Indian contractors beat the Irish medical fraternity fairly easily and a Dr Robert Maris made thirty runs.

There was a big party at the British club after the game and most of the competitors from the four teams were present and enjoying the occasion.

Copping spent a long time drinking and chatting to his look alike, Wally Wright, and they became firm friends. But they were not to know that their similarities would prove to be disadvantageous as time went on.

Watching the game was Leila and her sister, and she made sure to make herself known to Copping. He had not seen her for a while and it seemed both were withdrawn from each other, as though the spark had diminished over time.

Copping made an effort to be friendly, he kissed her both cheeks when they got close, and held her affectionately, but during the past few weeks he had tried to get his social life in check. The pressure from O'Byrne was not ceasing and it was having an effect on his mentality, so he thought it was time to stop leading with his chin.

Chapter 19

A new responsibility

Autumn/Winter 1984

Over the next few days, he started to felt guilty, his mind was occupied with his upcoming date with Leila rather than his work. He pretended to keep his head down, while his mind was tormented.

At the end of the week, he received an instruction from Mahmoud to stop by his office. When he arrived, his secretary had already gone home, so he knocked and waited.

"Come in, the door is open."

Mahmoud was busy writing at his desk and did not look up for some time. "Well, sit down, Mr Copping, this will not take long."

Copping sat down with caution, he had known Mahmoud long enough to know that he could show discontent in a second, so he chose to be withdrawn and let his boss do the talking. Being that he was a big man with a very loud voice, Copping felt it best to remain silent and wait.

"Mr Copping, I hope that you are well."

"Yes sir, thank you."

"That's good, and when I was away those four weeks, I hope that my deputy Mr Masri looked after you." Copping remembered that Masri was somehow connected to O'Byrne so said nothing untoward.

"Yes sir, he did, but you know," Copping began testing his luck, "I noticed that the potted plants in his office were all blooming and yet your plants here are withering."

"What are you trying to say, Mr Copping?"

"Only, Mr Mahmoud, that our Prince Charles back in the United Kingdom advises that we all should talk quietly to our plants, and they will respond with flowers and growth if we are kind to them. But with noise and aggression, they just wither and die…"

There was a pause, then Mahmoud relaxed and appreciated the joke, "Yes Mr Copping, then that is the case with me, and when you see my plants grow high you will know our projects are doing well. Right now, they reflect that things are not so good."

"That's a good point, sir."

"That's why I have called you into my office at this time of the afternoon. It's because I want you to set up the management controls for all my projects, including Project 109, starting from now."

Copping kept quiet and waited.

"My team are very knowledgeable, they know the situation, but they do not react to my urgency. They need someone who is not familiar, and one that will push them and still hold respect. You are this man."

"Thank you, Mr Mahmoud. I do try."

"I know that, and that's why I need you to report back to me on Project 109, but do so surreptitiously, you understand?"

"Absolutely, sir, and thank you for your confidence in me."

"OK Copping, that's all. Report to me every week at this time, I expect the first report next week."

"Thank you. Mr Mahmoud. I will do that, but I may have to cut my visits to Basra until this is done."

"Do what you have to do, I'll see you in a week."

"Thank you, sir." He rose and quickly exited the office.

As he walked down the corridor, he was relieved Mahmoud had not taken offense in regard to the plant.

A few days later.

After his first visit to Project 109, he pondered over the experience he had with the Italians not to say of the ghastly coat he had to put over his head for security during the trip.

He thought all would be normal after removing the coat once Gorgis had stopped the car but this was not the case, because he was confronted by a monstrosity of a building, it seemed to him that they were in the Photo shoot for a western film. The building was similar to an old western army fort, with a large log gate. The whole structure was square, the walls made from halved tree trunks and it reminded him so much of the old pioneering days, to think that this may be his home for a couple of days was exhilarating.

The gates at the entrance were huge and erected in the same design as the walls, at least six or seven metres high, and a small inspection hatch was in the centre of the gates.

Gorgis honked the horn of the car, the small hatch opened, and a man could be seen peering from the inside. He spoke in Italian and neither of them could understand what he said.

Gorgis stroked his moustache, then swung out of the door and shouted up to the face at the window.

"I am Gorgis al-Mubarak and I work for the department of oil in Baghdad."

The voice said, "So?"

"We have to work here for two days and your project director has given us permission to stay here."

"No one outside of our team is allowed to stay in this compound, you must find somewhere else to stay. Good night."

And with that, the window slammed shut.

"But we're in the middle of the bloody desert, Gorgis, there is nowhere to stay, and after seven hours in the car I'm knackered. I must sleep."

"Yes, yes. I understand, I will knock again and ring the bell. We'll force them to let us speak with their camp commander."

After ten minutes of continuous knocking, the window opened again.

"We've told you to go away and find somewhere else, there is no room." The man at the window spoke English and sounded impatient.

"I want to speak with the camp commander, now please."

The man left the window open and moved out of sight, then after about five minutes another face appeared, seeming more positive than his predecessor.

"I understand you want accommodation for two days?"

"Yes, we have permission from your director, and we have the consignment letter here." He lifted the letter up to show the commander.

"OK, you can stay here for one night only, it's impossible for you to stay longer as I have additional men coming tomorrow."

The gate opened and they drove through to an open courtyard. Inside there were four or five land cruisers parked neatly around the perimeter.

A man in formal field army dress then came and met them, with another man alongside him.

"My name is Callow, Barry Callow, I'm the commander of the fort. Welcome." He gestured towards the other person next to him, "This is Popham, he is the orderly and will take you to your quarters. You can have a meal in the mess hall but you'd better hurry, it finishes at 18:30. I am sorry we can only offer you one night's stay, there must have been some sort of misunderstanding when the accommodation was requested."

Callow started to turn, then as if as an afterthought added, "By the way gentleman, this is a classified area, so please do not attempt to talk with others in the camp. They have been instructed not to talk or mix with anybody whilst in Iraq. Good night and good luck."

He shook hands with both Gorgis and Copping, who then returned to the car to pick up their belongings.

The next day.

The Italian's hospitality stopped with the commander. At the evening meal the resident Italians ignored them completely and kept themselves within their own community.

In the morning, Gorgis and Copping had difficulty taking a shower as the cubicle was so small that it was difficult to manoeuvre your way in or out without hitting each of the sides. But it was better than nothing, and they both persevered.

After breakfast, the two boarded the car and drove around the site to make an overall assessment. It would need to be done quickly as with only one day available to them, time was of the essence. Later, they would need to drive back to Baghdad and had decided that this should be done in the cool of the night. Copping groaned and thought, *with a bloody coat over my head.*

*****

The work was seen to be progressing, albeit behind schedule, and Copping rolled some ideas around in his head regarding acceleration methods. To assist in this, he reviewed the drawings and assessed how many men could work safely in each area effectively. Once he had done this, he evaluated the logic of construction, then ensured that materials and detailed drawings were available to complete the work.

After collecting enough information to carry out his study, he returned to the car where Gorgis was sitting quietly and said, "Time to go, my friend."

Now suitably hooded, Copping had plenty to think about, and his mind was on the grandeur of the bunker, a magnificent design. When finished, it would be completely hidden beneath the desert sands.

The strength of the roof structure was designed to take the weight of armoured vehicles and to withstand the power of missile strikes. There was even a dummy village to be built on top of the crescent shaped roof.

Copping was aware that he knew more now than he should, and party members would continually watch his movements. He also realised that his life may be in danger, not so much now as later, when the work was finished.

The South Koreans were not a security risk, they did not mix with anyone and could not communicate with others due to the language difficulties and the silence law imposed for overseas workers.

When they returned home to Korea, the ruling regime would ensure silence, and as for the small band of Italians, Copping wondered whether these guys were part and parcel of the Casa Nostra, where it is their given right to swear allegiance to the cause.

Although he was inquisitive regarding the location of the bunkers, it was something that he should not contemplate, as knowing its position would compromise his own safety. If the Ba'ath party found he was working on map co-ordinates, it would be a death sentence. He would probably end on the banks of the Tigris one Friday morning, only this time he would not be the onlooker.

Chapter 20

A Small Country

In the world of international commerce, it is difficult to know the boundaries of decency. If a salesman pulls off a major deal, his company stands to make a huge profit. The salesman himself would also expect a sizable bonus.

The chain of procurement in the sale of arms is difficult to justify, it is obscene to think of profit made from hurt and killing! How many company personnel have a conscience once the deal is made, especially when two months later their product may kill many people.

Their excuse will always be 'If I didn't close the deal, then someone else would have done.'

Iraq, 1983–1985.

At this time, the Ba'ath party were intent on the purchase of a raw nuclear fuel from a source in Africa. It was a banned substance and illegal to buy without a license.

But Saddam believed everything has a price, so to negotiate this and arrange procurement, there was no better organisation then the Italian Mafia to carry out the work.

The Ba'ath party made their initial contact with the group in Sicily early on in 1983, and later the organisation set up a project office in Vatican City. This would provide adequate cover that was needed to pull this trade off without the rest of the world knowing.

An Iraqi envoy under the cover of 'world peace' set up his office in Vatican City and this initiation of the establishment was not expected to draw unnecessary attention.

The Mafia would then broker a deal to purchase and ship the product Saddam wanted. The cargo would be disguised, and all documents would show a Vatican insignia, all of which would be controlled by the Vatican office.

However, the Italians were providing Iraq with questionable equipment, including chemical engineering facilities and laser-enriched uranium, throughout the war period.

The CIA soon discovered that the financial arrangements for the illegal purchase of uranium was been carried out right under their noses by an Italian bank in the US, which had raised over $4 billion in loans.

December 1984.

Early in December, Copping took a walk outside of the Sheraton hotel for some exercise. He had stepped out in a light cheque jacket and dark navy-coloured trousers, his shirt was open at the neck, but he soon noticed the icy cold wind blowing from the east and it wasn't long before he returned to the foyer and wandered over to the bar.

Sat in his normal spot, was his friend JP, smoking a cigarette and reading a book. He looked up and smiled as Copping approached.

They shook hands in a polite greeting and JP opened up the conversation, "I'm glad that I bumped into you! I have something to ask. Did you know that I was schooled in Lebanon?" He didn't wait for Copping to answer. "Well today, I came across an old friend who is actually the Italian ambassador in Iraq, he's living here and has invited us over to his house for drinks later if you're up for it?"

"Is this formal or informal?" asked Copping.

"Casual, shirt and trousers for him. Although his wife is a snob, might be better to dress up rather than down."

Two hours later.

Copping reached out and rang the doorbell of a massive, private house. They were greeted by a rounded jovial man, wearing an open neck checked shirt, and although the bottom half was hanging over his belt, he was the sort of person that always looked good, no matter how badly they are dressed. More importantly, he had a big welcoming smile.

After they entered the house, they all sat down for some snacks and at around midday, he asked the butler to serve some cocktails. His wife, who had just joined them, showed her annoyance that alcohol was being served. She soon disappeared into the main part of the house, and Copping had the opinion that she was the social climber behind the brains.

Vincenso, the ambassador, was a surprisingly different sort of man. He was cheerful, unpretentious and full of joy, he entertained in the most unassuming way and showed his skills playing an eight stringed guitar.

Sophie, his wife, had long left the group, and it seemed she was now disgusted with her husband. They were all continuing to drink alcohol, so she must have thought that Copping and JP were a bad influence.

Vincenso only put down his drink and stopped playing when the phone rang. It was the Italian consulate, apparently asking if he could raise a special case Italian visa.

"A diplomatic visa? They must be someone of great importance," said JP, his interest peaked.

"Well yes, but I cannot remember his name." Vincenso moved to a nearby desk and rummaged through a sheaf of papers.

"Argh! Yes, here we are," as if speaking to himself, he continued, "Mr Zahawe, and he will be based in the Vatican, not Italy as such. Now, whom do I phone to verify this." he quipped.

JP did not let him off the hook and went on, "Will he be the Italian envoy based in the Vatican that I hear about?"

"I think he may be, but look, my friends, you must excuse me as this is especially important. I think the Pope may want to use him as a courier to bring peace between the two countries, but this is only my interpretation, so please be discreet with this information."

"Of course, Vincenzo, when you're less busy we must get together again, and thanks for the recital."

Six months later.

In a small village just south of Bari in southern Italy, a band of ageing men were sipping coffee in a café. They were only yards from the quayside and could hear the sea lapping against the rocks just below them.

In this party of five, four of them looked uncomfortable, and it was these four who seemed overdressed in crisp white shirts and dark trousers, with immaculately polished shoes. Two of the four had white hair, one with a ponytail, whilst the other two were balding.

The fifth member of the party, called Alphonso, was dressed in a faded blue t-shirt and jeans and was doing most of the talking. Those listening said nothing but nodded their heads in unison.

"Thank you all for travelling today to attend this meeting. I'm sure you'll agree that what I have to say will bring our organisation some good business." He went on, "It is not always wise to enter into a new deal without having intimate knowledge of the subject you're about to invest in." He paused. "Iraq are in the market to buy some interesting arms. They have oil and will deal with anyone as long as the business is done discreetly. Most of their equipment is regulated and controlled under international law, but some of it is not, and this is where we come in."

Those in attendance were in deep thought, each one thinking of the benefits to their organisation.

"Gentlemen, as you know, we're willing to carry out activities inside or outside of any regulations, and it *always* pays more for anything illegal."

"What exactly is the job you are talking about?" Paulo, a healthy looking sixty-three-year-old, was inquisitive.

"The answer is complicated but, in essence, it's a case of acquiring basic nuclear unrefined material from Niger and delivering to Iraq without detection."

He continued, "We'll act as the middlemen between the two countries, but we need to avoid the problems that are expected with international authorities. This may mean a bribe, or perhaps a tactical plan that I will propose later."

"Tactical plan?" asked Luigi.

"Yes, I'll explain as simply as possible. We buy two loads of the substance and deliver them at different times on different routes, then if one is held up, the other still has a chance of being delivered. Each consignment will have a veiled 'consignment note' and 'bill of laden.'"

Alphonso ran his steel-like eyes around the group of the men assembled and continued in a monotone voice, "This material is called 'Yellow Cake' and it is an unrefined but radioactive material that has been leached from the parent metal." He paused again. "In its raw state it cannot be used directly as an incendiary device, but is better refined and used as a secondary one." Once again, he scanned those in the group.

Luigi, a younger member of the organisation, was becoming excited as this seemed like an interesting prospect. "Your appraisal, Alphonso, is fascinating, but what's in it for our organisation?"

"Niger is one of the poorest countries, if not the poorest in the world, yet they have the most valuable element that may be the single most important item for a country that's losing a war!"

He continued, "We can make a good deal with the Africans, and Saddam will pay top bucks for this supply."

"What are the quantities involved?" Luigi enquired.

"I would say for the first move, about two thousand kilos."

"Sounds good to me and I'll be interested in more like this, especially if we can get a good deal."

"If he agrees at the meeting, I will inform the Don and then we can arrange the purchase and transportation. Although, I will need your assistance regarding the proposed cut across each of your territories." Alphonso was very direct.

"Raise your hands if you believe we should proceed."

All five hands were raised.

"That makes it easy then. We are now in the Nuclear Industry."

Paulo was the one of the quieter men at the meeting, who was hesitant before raising his hand, but he eventually worked up the courage to ask Alphonso, "Where is the Don based for this one?"

Alphonso looked back at him with a hard glare. "He is working from home, but the operation will be run from a property within Vatican City, and an Iraqi ambassador will head this up. Although, his position is to boost international goods, so it will be between the Ba'ath party in Iraq and us."

He paused and took a deep breath, "There is one thing more that I will require an agreement on and it's something that is necessary to keep the peace with our neighbours. After all, there is enough in it for all of us."

He paused again for a minute. "For this operation we will need to join forces with our brothers, the Camorra and Ndrangheta, and you must understand that the business will be shared. At our next meeting we'll have representatives from each of these organisations."

Each man raised his hand in agreement, they knew these conditions were not to be questioned.

Alphonso ordered more drinks from the bar, and the five men relaxed, talking amongst themselves about local gossip in their region and the wellbeing of their families.

After about an hour, the group broke up, their transport was waiting outside the restaurant. Each of the five cars drove away at ten-minute intervals.

Chapter 21

A Time to not tell anything

Spring 1985

Copping's spare time was at a premium, he simply did not have enough of it.

It seemed that his social priorities would need to be scheduled carefully, and the first activity concerned the importance of maintaining the Meridian tennis reservation book. This book provided the information that O'Byrne required and Copping needed the time to maintain it this, something else would need to go as this was his lifeline.

O'Byrne continued to press Copping, and it was starting to annoy him, he wanted a break. Then, one afternoon O'Byrne arrived at the hotel unexpectedly, wanting to talk, and would not take 'No' for an answer. Their meeting ended in stalemate as Copping was not prepared to open up his knowledge regarding the work associated with Project 109 (the bunker earmarked for storage of WMD)

O'Byrne left Copping and he was not happy with his discussions with Copping as he felt there was something he was not telling him!

*****

In the meantime, Copping was being forced into spending more time with the engineers on site, it was the source of his report to Mahmoud.

He grilled them on a weekly basis and the information he received was always consistent and accurate. Copping was a foreigner, a mercenary in a country with unfortunate circumstances, and he always made a point of being honest with his meetings with Mahmoud.

The two main contractors for the construction work had been carefully selected, with the Italians carrying out design and engineering, and the North Koreans working the construction. Each were chaperoned on site at the beginning of the day, and chaperoned back to the departure point at the end of the day. The importance of maintaining secrecy was inviolable. Copping was in the middle, sitting on a knife edge, and if anything was leaked, his head would be on the block.

*****

Copping's weekly drives with Gorgis to the bunker were always daunting, and the journey was long and hot. He now insisted himself that he always wear a blindfold, it was his own assurance policy, he would make sure he never knew the location of the bunker, and he would make sure those around him were aware of his preventative action.

Chapter 22

A Visit From a Friend.

Spring/Summer 1985

Copping arrived back at his hotel at midday on a Thursday. He was extremely tired and particularly looking forward to the weekend and a rest. But as he approached the rotating doors there was a problem, he realised there were too many people in the vicinity, it was making things uncomfortable just trying to access his room.

It was one thing moving with difficulty on the ground floor, and another finding a lift to take you up to your level, he was wondering why everything was so hectic.

Copping was glad to reach the peace and quiet of his room. It was cool when he entered and the sun was shining through the blinds, reflecting its rays on the carpet. He opened the blinds, then the sliding doors to the outside balcony, a rush of hot air passed him. He preferred this to the cool refrigerated-type of air associated with air conditioning. From the fridge, he withdrew an Iraqi bottle of beer, and his first gulp of the ice-cold liquid slipped down his throat into his stomach, cooling his body. He emptied the bottle in a few minutes and moved to find another when the phone rang.

"Is that you Edward? This is Safiya."

Copping was glad to hear her voice, he thought she had given up on him, but now his heart jumped a beat. He began to feel guilty about his date with Leila.

"Where are you? I've been worried." It was the truth, as each night he envisioned different scenarios of how she might get into trouble with the authorities.

"I'm fine, I've just been busy. My ward was submerged with soldiers suffering from chemical backfire from our own military assaults." She continued, "I'm not experienced in war wounds and needed to learn quickly how to deal with such horror." She paused for a moment before she proceeded, "If you're not busy, perhaps I can come over and see you as I have the rest of the day off."

"Of course, Safiya, perhaps I can meet you in the foyer?"

"No, I am by myself this time and will come to your room. I have checked your location, and it's only one floor up the escalator."

"OK, I'll leave the door open."

One hour later.

Safiya cautiously approached Copping's room, slipped in, and closed the door silently behind her. Her smile was radiant as she moved elegantly over the floor and hugged Copping as he rose from the chair. It was the first sign of affection she had shown since he had met her, and he welcomed it.

She wore a pink shirt with the collar riding nicely over the lapels of a light coat. He was trembling with emotion as he moved closer to her, but she was not moving, she stood absolutely still. Her arms were hanging down by her side as if she was waiting for him to hold her, and in a moment, he slid his arms over her shoulders, then raised his right hand behind her neck and gently eased her towards him. Their faces were almost touching, and their eyes were focused on each other.

The air conditionings quiet hum was the only noise in the room, it was a moment held in time. Gently he brought her face to his and they kissed avidly, sharing the same unashamed passion, as he guided her to the bed. Her topcoat fell, followed by his shirt, and soon a pile of clothes littered the floor. In that moment they forsook the rules of the Ba'ath party, too caught up in one another to comprehend the severity of their actions.

A little later, Copping stirred, he gently stroked Safyia's short curly hair, it was like silk. She looked up.

"Are you married, Edward?"

"No. I was some years ago, but the marriage failed, and we were divorced."

"Why did it fail?"

"She left me for another man."

"I too was married, and that also failed, so we are both failures."

They both laughed, but then she was serious again, although it did not deter her charm.

"May I ask where your husband is now?" Copping was intrigued but did not want to ruin their moment by making her uncomfortable.

"He was Lebanese and a dissident, like me, and was jailed for his actions."

"Do you mean he was demonstrating?"

"Yes, but nothing serious. But as he was a foreigner, the party jailed him. They're like animals, all of them, and I hate them!" She was silent for a while and then said, "I've been lucky so far, I got a very good medical degree that warrants me to practice in Baghdad, whilst others with slightly lesser grades go to the war front. And now I have witnessed the horrible injuries to our soldiers, and our wards are swamped with the 'lucky ones' that *may* survive!"

Both were silent for some minutes, each with their own thoughts, before Safiya quietly spoke. "My husband sadly died last year. He did not return to Lebanon."

She quickly changed the subject. "Some of the wounded men, that is those that are well enough to talk, told me that the Iraqi officers would shoot them in the back if they stalled a charge. Many of our men died at the hands of their brother officers."

Nothing was said after that, they both lay with their own thoughts and took comfort in being close to one another. After a while, the mood lightened and they discussed life in Ireland, having light-hearted banter. When they finally broke away from each other, Copping got up and excused himself, and started to make his way to the bathroom.

He had moved only two strides when the doorbell rang and they both froze, their joy quickly turning into fear.

After his initial panic, he pulled on his clothes and began adjusting himself as he walked slowly to the door. The bell rang again.

Safiya whispered, "Just one more minute!" So he stalled a second more, and glancing over his shoulder he asked, "Ready?"

"Ready," she answered quickly.

When he opened the door, three men were standing menacingly outside. One, who was dressed smartly in a dark suit, stood the closest, whilst the man on his right just stared, saying nothing. The third man stood behind, hands crossed in front of him and legs astride. Copping looked at each in turn, looking directly into their intently serious faces.

"My name is Mustafa, I am the head of security in this hotel and these are my assistants. You must know Mr Copping, that local visitors must not mix with foreigners outside of business. These rules are very serious, especially when it comes to local females in a foreigner's hotel rooms." He paused, then continued sternly, "Also, it's Friday, our day of prayer."

He looked past Copping, into the room behind him, and his gaze found Safiya. By this time, she was casually sitting on a chair, and though her appearance was ruffled, this was not as noticeable as her charm. Smiling and smoking a cigarette, she asked Jamal politely in Arabic, "Do you want me to accompany you downstairs, Mr Mustafa?" She was teasing him, and this mischievous gesture could land her in even more danger.

"Yes madam, if you please. We need to find out what your business was with Mr Copping."

He beckoned Safiya and at first, she ignored him, sat for a few moments and puffed her cigarette. Then, rising slowly, she walked straight out of the door, and one of the two men escorted her down the corridor, out of sight.

Mustafa and the other man waited until Copping left the room, slamming the door behind him, before they followed in the same direction as Safiya.

"Now, Mr Copping, you have some explaining to do. We'll talk in the interview room." He gestured towards the lift, "It's in the basement, under the reception."

Oh yes, thought Copping, *the same room where I found Tom Patten, sitting naked, waiting for the scud to explode above him.* He started to worry. *There has to be a way I can get out of this.*

The area of the bunker where they were situated was basic, originally designed to protect patrons during air strikes and missiles, but now used as an interrogation centre.

It was the crudest part of this luxury hotel. The concrete foundations and superstructure were clearly visible, but the finish was rough. It was not a place of safety, but a place of fear.

Copping was told to sit on a concrete bench, which was terribly uncomfortable. He thought again of Tom Patten, sitting on the same bench. Though this time it was not a missile problem, it was Safiya's honour that was at stake.

Mustafa stood in front of him and instructed one of his assistants to lock the door. This alarmed Copping, and he began to expect the worst.

He switched off the main lights, and then positioned another local light that beamed into Copping's eyes.

"I'm sorry for this inconvenience, Mr Copping, but I would remind you that you have overstepped your authority, you have also disrespected the rules of our country. In particular, you have been found cavorting with a professional Iraqi and this meeting with the young lady earlier should never have happened without permission from our party beforehand."

Copping felt uncomfortable, the terms in his contract clearly stipulated he should not talk or mix with locals outside of his working day.

"I *do* understand why foreigners should not mix with the local people, it's to protect the country from unnecessary gossip, but I assure you, Mr Mustafa, that we have been careful not to talk politics on this or any other occasion."

"Do you expect me to believe this? It seems you're not taking our situation seriously, Mr Copping."

Copping tried to clarify his situation. "I met this lady," speaking as though he had no personal attachment to Safiya, "at the hospital whilst trying to book a medical examination and we became friends. Our conversation was amicable. You see, we've both been divorced and share the same loneliness. I reiterate Mr Mustafa, we didn't discuss any politics that would be considered detrimental to your party, we didn't discuss politics at all."

"Is your lady friend a medical doctor?"

"Yes, she is."

"Then she should know better than to mix with a foreigner."

"I understand, sir." Copping felt threatened and did not want to get Safiya into trouble, he did not know where she had been taken after she left the room.

There was silence for a moment and Copping could hear water dripping in the background. The sound of the water hitting the floor echoed against the concrete walls and he shivered.

Copping heard Mustafa turn away and when he looked up the Iraqi was staring at the ground, it seemed he was working out what to say next.

The man standing behind Mustafa shuffled on the stone floor, but was out of Copping's sight, and he began fearfully anticipating a violent blow. Copping had heard that this was the way interrogations started, but it did not materialise. A few minutes later, Mustafa switched the light on and glared at Copping, who breathed a sigh of relief.

"This matter is not closed, Mr Copping, and you should not talk to anyone else about this matter, except the Party Member that you are required to work with. He will be notified in due course and direct you accordingly."

Chapter 23

The Doctor's Demise

Autumn 1985

The intervention at the hotel did not deter Safiya. She cared little for the police, or the state. They were simply carrying out their job as required and she was simply trying to live a free life, but in an authoritarian country.

It was now evening, and she sat with a book at the window of her hospital accommodation. Across the room from her sat her close friend Maisha, who was thoroughly enjoying listening to the story of what happened at the hotel. Safiya fully explained how serious the guards were when carrying out such a trivial duty. Maisha laughed, "It took three large men to break you two up, there must have been something really serious going on…"

Safiya blushed and added, "Don't even think about that, my friend!"

Maisha was lying back, looking at the ceiling, thinking of her student days. "You know, Safiya, I enjoyed Edinburgh so much. Life was so free and the students just partied constantly. Looking back at those times, I really can't imagine hotel security being concerned about two adults talking in a room." There was silence. Then Maisha added, "You were only talking, weren't you?'

"If we weren't, what would security do to us in Scotland?"

"Depends on what you were doing," laughed Maisha.

"But say we were making love? What then?" asked Safiya with a giggle.

Maisha flushed, "I guess the Scottish police wouldn't care, it's less important in the UK. Taking drugs on the other hand—"

The telephone interrupted them.

Safiya lifted the receiver and after the caller was talking for a few minutes, her eyes hardened, her body stiffened, and she put the phone back on the hook.

"What is it Safiya? Is anything wrong?" Maisha enquired.

Safiya returned to her seat, her mind had to assess the situation before she explained it to Maisha.

"It seems I am being reprimanded."

"How?"

"I'm to join an operations unit for my sins. The correction officer advised me it's for training purposes, and that they'll tell me what career options will be available to me later."

Safiya paused. "Can you imagine, Maisha, she mentioned trauma study."

"Is this move going to be good for you? Can you return to your original specialist aspirations at al-Kindy should you want to?" Maisha was desperate for answers. She was worried for Safiya, who was her closest friend, as they both knew this move may be detrimental for her.

"They said that they'll review the situation every three months." She was deflated, but still strong, and sat in silence for a few minutes deep in thought, then brightened.

"Maisha, my dear friend, I must prepare for my journey to Basra tomorrow, but I'll write and let you know how I am." Her face told the story as she turned away to pack her bags.

Chapter 24

A Journey to Hell

Winter 1985

It was dark when Safiya was carrying her little bag of clothes and boarded a bus for Jazair, a town close to Al Qurna. The journey was expected to take just over two hours and the other people in the bus consisted of six male nurses, two of whom were older than Safiya, and the rest were military officers.

Safiya sat and looked out of the window, but as dawn broke the sun was hot and bright, and she needed to move to the other set of seats opposite her to ease the situation. Graciously, two of the military men saw her discomfort and swapped seats with her.

It was late in the year and the weather was cool outside, so after a while she settled down with a book. After driving for about an hour, the bus pulled over and the driver was talking frantically to the senior officer on board.

"We cannot go further, sir, I've heard on the radio that the Iranians have penetrated the marshes using small boats and are heading for Al Qurna."

The intercom radio on the bus was old and the reception was not good, but the news could be understood through the cackle of interference.

The driver was getting more worried. "They've used helicopter gunships to destroy the sixth army battalion and are now heading towards Al Qurna and Umm Qsar."

Up until this point, Safiya was not paying close attention, but now she listened intently to the two men discussing the radio report.

The officer turned to the driver, with his back upright and his jaw set. "We go to Jazair and we await orders from base."

"But s—!" the officer stopped him.

"You have my instructions. We drive to Jazair and wait."

The six military men retreated to the back of the bus and were trying to contact their headquarters using field phones, but the reception was poor, and they struggled to get a connection.

In the approach to Al Qurna, the senior officer ordered the driver to divert and take a lesser road to the east. Their new destination was Basra.

During the journey, they stopped on a number of occasions, whenever overhead aircrafts were heard, but none of them troubled them and they carried on.

On the outskirts of Basra, the old bus pulled into an army field barracks and parked in an open area some way from the accommodation buildings. There were many military vehicles parked in the area, including armoured cars, ambulances, jeeps, buses and four Iraqi T-72 tanks, and the place was awash with troops.

Safiya felt scared and alone, she was estranged from her family and her only close friends. She knew she could not talk to anyone, so she stood there, shivering in the November night air.

The officer spoke to the medics on board and asked them to remain seated while he found out what is happening. A few minutes later, he returned and said he would address the group.

"Doctors Hamdi, Jawaerl and Mahdi will remain here until further orders are given, and all nurses will report to the hospital unit which is on the west side of the block. I suggest you go there and enquire if they need medical assistance. You should seek out the third battalion, I understand they need your help urgently."

"What's the problem, Captain?" Safiya asked politely.

"The Iranians have attacked from the east. At first our generals thought they were trying to secure the highway, but we think this is a feint and the main target is the town of Al-Faw, at the tip of the peninsula. If they're successful in capturing it, this will cut us off from the gulf."

He went on, "They're said to be attacking from the southern marshes using speed boats with pontoon bridges, our orders are to stem the attacks from the east. A truck has been sent to pick us up—" The officer broke off, he had received a call and moved away for confidential reasons.

Earlier that day, the weather had been warm and the sky was clear, but suddenly it changed and soon the rain started, and it was torrential. Large areas started to flood and the vehicles parked on grass were finding it difficult to move.

"Will we lose access to the gulf?" one of the nurses asked.

"I hope not, but we have many casualties already and you may be working an extended shift, so please be prepared for this."

For the first time, Safiya felt distressed. She was alone and the noise of battle was getting closer. Jets were screaming overhead and she could hear the sound of large calibre guns.

Four hours later.

Safiya was ordered to join the third Battalion and was lucky to find a truck nearly full of third Battalion soldiers amidst all the mayhem. She managed to get a seat, but there were so many soldiers that there was no way she could feel comfortable. Her understanding was that she was due to join the third Battalion, although they were under pressure earlier from the enemy and had actually been driven back. Luckily, things had stabilised on both sides in the process of digging in.

She overheard an officer saying that the Iraqis had held advance but had lost the peninsula at Al-Faw.

The truck was overflowing with troops, so she had to stand for three hours, crushed up against soldiers that were in full battledress and armed. Her hands and feet were cold and her head was wedged against a soldier's back. It made things worse that she could not see the direction the truck was going in. The ride was very bumpy, and the rain continued to lash down. Then, when the wind changed direction, it blew in through the canopy and she got wet through to the skin.

After about twenty minutes, she remembered that the captain gave her instructions on a piece of paper and she frantically searched her pockets. It was difficult as with each bend the soldiers pressed against her and she could not move her arms. Sometime later she managed to free the paper instructions from her coat and read what was on it.

Regiment: Third battalion
Officer in charge: Lieutenant Jawaarl
Set up: Mobile medical unit
Categorise patients as deceased (morgue), minor (re-engage), major (incapacitated), procedure (immediate surgery). Certify where appropriate.

The atmosphere started to change as they approached where the fighting was worst, the noise was now just short of deafening. Two tanks were in line close by and firing salvo after salvo, the machine gun was continuous and relentless. Then there were the injured, many of whom were screaming, while others were asking for their mothers. Safiya thought most of the soldiers were at least ten years younger than she was.

The air was thick with sand, like a fog. It was a picture of destruction one moment, then nothing but fog and noise the next.

Safiya was confused and did not know whether to lie down, crouch, or run, but she knew she was here for a reason and needed to stay calm. Her first duty was to set up a medical centre, so she shouted at a soldier who was sitting close by. She did not know what his duties were nevertheless he responded and stood to attention.

"Come with me. Now." His instincts soon took over and within a few minutes he had erected an enclosure, behind what looked like a cow barn. Together they set up makeshift operating tables, and in silence he marked out four areas in close proximity of the enclosure.

The noise was overwhelming, there were shells exploding within a few hundred yards and pieces of metal, wood and other debris were falling onto them, and all while the rain was causing the canvas roof of the enclosure to droop.

Her assistant, the soldier she had recruited, never stopped working. One moment he was labouring over the structure of the enclosure, the next he was holding medical instruments for the injured.

The four designated areas, so carefully sectioned off earlier, were quickly forgotten. The dead, the minor injuries, those waiting for surgery, and those waiting for transport, were all together. Rashid, the helpful soldier, called in four other soldiers from the infantry battalion and they split the work. Two of them cleared the deceased to an area some fifty yards away, moving the bodies of their brothers carefully, laying each one in line with the previous, a note pinned to the blanket identified them.

Safiya had little field surgical experience, and certainly no actual field trauma expertise, but she dealt with each patient meticulously, whether it was setting a bone, amputating a leg, or stitching a hole in a man's body. In a normal operating theatre the work may have been carried out differently, but there were no complaints that evening, or the next, or the one after that.

Her apron and overalls were covered with blood and dust. There was even a time when she could do nothing for one of the soldiers. And yet, she was very patient with him, taking her time as she administered morphine and made sure he was comfortable, before ensuring he was taken to the main field hospital.

*****

Ambulances were screaming in and out all day and night, taking the worst of the injured back to the main hospital for attention. By this point, Safiya and her five orderlies were beyond exhaustion.

Nearly all soldiers that came for attention had post-traumatic stress. Some of them were without physical injury but she kept them for observation, because she could see the fear in their eyes, the fear of being sent back to the slaughter. In most cases where it was appropriate, she recommended the man return home for recuperation, and she would smile to herself for those going home. Just looking at them, she knew that most were only boys who were hardly out of the school playground.

Safiya made a day bed inside the enclosure, and whenever possible she lay down for a nap, even for a few minutes. It was an effort to stay awake for those hours. Rashid and the two nurses did the same, trying to take their rests in a shift-like pattern, but they were often too exhausted to stick to it.

Three weeks later.

Safiya was trying to ignore her fatigue while working on a patient, when she heard the deafening explosion. The battalion positions had been attacked by two phantom jets and had to withdraw from their current position in order to seek better protection. During the assault, the phantoms fired air-to-ground missiles, killing seventeen soldiers.

One hour later.

The area was strafed by a helicopter gunship, before it was shot down by an Iraqi air to ground missile that killed a further sixty soldiers.

Either by luck or better judgement, none of the medical staff and orderlies were killed or injured. This could have been due to the fast action of Rashid and his orderlies, because at the first sound of the aircrafts, they were able to quickly move the entire enclosure to a place of relative safety.

During and after the raid, Safiya never left the side of her patients, always ensuring they were comfortable and that they had necessary dressings and drip-feeds, despite the fear and chaos around her.

But she was now working on borrowed time. She was told she would be withdrawn later that day but did not wait to find out when. Instead, she found a truck that was due to depart to the field depot, climbed into the back, and fell asleep.

Note
During the last four years of war, both sides had lost nearly a million lives but the Iranians, with help from an Israeli loan of $200 million, had swung the balance of the war in their favour. During the year of 1985, they launched an attack called Operation Dawn V, it was a plan to split Iraq into two halves. The ingenious part was their intention to use flat bottom assault boats on the Iraqi marshes and surprise the Iraqi third corps based in Al Qurna, about eighty miles from Baghdad.

The balance was expected to swing even more in Iran's favour after the assault, but Saddam relied on his chemical weapons and held off the enemy east of the town on the peninsula north of al-Al-Faw

Chapter 25

No Rest for the Wicked

December 1985 – February 1986.

The assumptions that the captain had made prior to the recent hostilities turned out to be correct, the enemy's main aim was to capture the peninsula north of the town of Al-Faw. The geography of this area is such that the Shatt-al-Arab waterway divides Iran to the North, and Iraq to the south. The town of Al-Faw is in the Iraqi section and its position is close to the southern tip.

The Iranians were now crossing the waterway on pontoon bridges after traversing the Iraqi marshes on flat bottom boats, and they were about to take over Al-Faw and a part Iraq that gives access to the Arabian Gulf.

Safiya had slept in the truck for an hour and was awakened by a soldier who was waiting to exit the truck.

A short while after he had left, she stood up and stretched her body, which ached considerably, and she still felt tired but certainly better than she had an hour or so before. She jumped down and suddenly noticed it was the location she had previously left when she first arrived from Baghdad.

Reaching the hospital entrance, she found it difficult get inside due to a two-way flow of people. Although she was clashing head on, she kept dodging as best she could, and at the same time looking for a command post where she could report for duty.

Suddenly a medic grabbed her hand. "Are you a doctor?"

She nodded.

"Come with me, our operating theatre is overwhelmed we need help."

She was beyond hungry and feeling weak, and she wanted to eat before she did anything, but there was no respite. She was pulled and pushed by the desperate medic until she found herself in a huge room. It was the biggest operating theatre she had ever seen. There were numerous beds placed around the periphery of the rectangular room, and each bed was in close proximity to the next, yet somehow the medics had enough space to squeeze between them to attend to the patients.

There were many soiled white coats, so it was difficult to differentiate between doctor, nurse and orderlies.

Once someone had finished with a patient, they were whisked away and another was put in their place, which was understood given that the queue of people waiting to be attended stretched outside the door.

An older man working carefully on an open stomach wound looked up and asked Safiya if she was a doctor, she nodded whilst he continued his work. A nurse next to him then asked her to watch the patient's vital statistics.

Thirty minutes later, the surgeon asked Safiya to stitch the wound, promising he would return to check how they were doing after he had attended the man in the next bed. Despite the fact this man's head was covered with lint and bandages, blood was already seeping out of the wound before the surgeon eased the gauze away from his head. Safiya commenced to finish the job that the surgeon had started.

She was slow but meticulous, and when she had finished the surgeon on the adjacent bed must have realised that she was new to trauma. He asked her to complete his work whilst he moved onto something more complicated. Another man's skin on both his left arm and leg had been ripped away, and her job was to remove all metal particles before sewing back what was left of his skin. She knew that he would need a graft, but she was not qualified for this procedure.

He remained inert throughout the operation, his head held high on the pillow and his eyes shut. Surprisingly, he showed no signs of discomfort, and the nurse only applied small doses of morphine intravenously, when appropriate.

The nurse turned to Safiya. "Please record his vital statistics and inform the surgeon if they change dramatically."

She was relieved that her duties would be within her remit. It also helped that the other surgeons working around her were supportive and continued to advise her on various procedures throughout the day.

Fifteen hours later.

Having lost count of her patients, Safiya's eyes began to close and her arms were dropping with fatigue.

A senior theatre surgeon eased up next to her, "Dr Mahdi, my name is Iqbal, I am the surgical theatre manager. Please take a break, I hope that you can get four hours rest, but I cannot guarantee as we have lost so many men." He sighed and added, as if an afterthought, "You will find a cot in the room adjourning, go before it is taken, I will finish up here."

She woke next morning on the floor of the dormitory, her cot was taken before she reached it the night before, so she took an alternative, the floor. She was stiff and grimy from a horrible night's sleep, and so decided to stand in line waiting for a vacant wash sink. She cleaned herself as well as she could, then looked for some food. There was nothing much to be found other than some meatballs and rice on a table outside the dormitory, but it would have to do.

A senior officer approached her. "You will be needed again in the field, on the north side of Al-Faw. Our troops have dug in, as have the Iranians. The two fronts are about a mile apart, and I would guess about five miles from the town of Al-Faw. At the moment, there is little action and only spasmodic fighting, although it seems there are still plenty of casualties." He smiled for the first time, "By the way, my name is Major Aziz."

"Major Aziz, thank you." Safiya was about to walk away, but then she looked down at her clothes, they were covered in filth. "Is it possible for me to change into something else? I lost my bag when travelling up from Baghdad."

"Speak to the local women, they may exchange clothes or give you fresh ones," he sighed, "but they may not be the best quality."

An hour later, with a black blouse, a long black skirt and an old shawl, Safiya set off for Al-Faw feeling tired but alive. It was only yesterday when she left the last hostilities and saw at least five hundred cadavers lying outside in the morgue. She began to wonder, *how much more of this war can I take?*

The truck approached the front line from the north as the Iranians were maintaining a line protecting what they had won in the last few days of fighting.

Although Safiya noticed it was now a lull on the front, both sides were recovering after such a devastating battle. Countless men had been lost on both sides over a large area and it had resulted in this, two opposing fronts both licking their wounds before the next nose-to-nose contest.

It was quieter than she had expected, nevertheless she felt fear amongst the men, with so many friends and relatives killed, it was always in their minds that they may be next. If it wasn't hand-to-hand combat, it may be a shell or an air attack, survival had become are rarity.

Iraq's front line was located in the middle of a salt factory, where some uninhabited buildings existed, a few of which were close to the Iranian front. Small bridges were also still intact and previously used by the workers to cross the salt flats.

The senior doctor instructed Safiya to appraise each of the injured soldiers, those still fit for duty would need to be returned to their units as soon as possible, and these replacements were essential due to drastic losses in the field.

For the third day running she was working a sixteen-hour day. Her duties were split between the operating theatre and the assessing office, and she maintained this schedule for a month. Her working days now extended to sleeping on site for four hours and working another twenty.

Overworked and tired, she inevitably fell ill. And although she tried to persevere, her condition prevailed due to her exhaustion, so she applied for a few days leave.

Having taken a rest, sitting on the corner of the medic enclosure, she was hoping a relief doctor would arrive, but instead a boy soldier rushed towards her from the direction of the front. "Doctor, doctor, please come quickly! A shell hit the building where I was sitting, there are people still inside, it's terrible, the men are screaming inside for help."

Two officers were studying a map on a temporary table close to Safiya, and one of them shouted to the boy asking him where the shell had exploded. The boy replied with the directions, but he gave no co-ordinates.

"Let's go," said the officer. "Doctor, please come with us, we may need you."

In just four hundred yards, they realised they had to cross a small bridge, where the road crossed the corner of the salt field, in order to reach the anticipated position. Immediately after the bridge, there was a crossroads and Safiya knew the direction they were heading was towards the Iranian front line.

The boy took the road straight ahead and the others, keeping their eyes on the boy, they did not look carefully up the adjacent roads. Then, just as they started to cross, there was a burst of machine gun fire, and one of the officers to her right dropped to the floor, groaning as he did so. The others held her back, stopping her running into the onslaught of gunfire. They all fell to the ground and soon after, the firing stopped. Safiya and the officer attended to the fallen man, his jacket was soaked in blood and Safiya removed it as quickly but as carefully as she could, attempting to stem the blood flow.

The two private soldiers who were with them moved silently along the adjacent road where the attack came from, stopping at every door and window, listening and looking. Once they reached the fifth door, the first soldier broke the door in, whilst the other opened fire through the window. They threw three grenades into the house and waited, but after the blasts there was total silence, so they continued to walk, checking the other houses as they went.

What followed was inconsistent firing and explosions. The boy that raised the alarm had continued running and was now out of sight.

Safiya continued to work on the fallen officer, she had cut open his chest and was working on the source of the blood loss. It seemed to have worked as the blood flow was stalling, and in a matter of minutes it had stopped.

An ambulance, called by the surviving officer, arrived and the medics continued where Safiya had left off, roaring off in a cloud of dust just minutes later.

Safiya was covered in blood from the open artery and was still in shock when, a few moments later, a jeep picked them up. The two soldiers, the surviving officer and herself got in the jeep and were driven back to camp.

There were still a few soldiers that required attention and after washing herself and finding some second-hand clothes, she continued her duties. It was another long, exhausting and debilitating day. She walked slowly to the chair she had sat in before the incident and sat down again. She could no longer hold back her tears, and bowing her head onto her chest, she sobbed. Her cries silenced the noise around her and those in earshot simply averted their eyes, they wanted to ensure that the doctor was not embarrassed.

That night she slept on her day bed, it was freezing cold and the rain continued all night, hitting the canvas above her and causing minor flooding. But all this did not matter.

At daybreak the next morning a jeep rolled up with a high-level officer and two men in plain clothes, they both had party bands around their arms, signifying their importance.

"Who is the commanding officer here?" one of them asked.

"I am." Lieutenant Jawaarl spoke up.

"My name is Shariq, I am the chairman of the Basra Ba'ath party, my colleague is Zaman, and the senior officer who accompanies us is Colonel Hadi. We have come to arrest a medic, a Doctor al-Mahdi"

"I am Mahdi." Safiya's voice sounded weak, even to her own ears.

"Doctor Safiya al-Mahdi, we're arresting you for 'overstepping your authority' and you will be escorted to the military prison in Basra where you will await your sentence."

"What is overstepping my authority? I've done nothing wrong."

"We have records to show that you have ordered the demobilisation of soldiers, the majority of whom were still capable of fighting for their country."

Jawaarl, the acting commanding officer, stepped up and introduced himself. "Doctor al-Mahdi is the bravest person that I've ever had the honour to work with, and it's not only me who can vouch for such a person, but the whole of this battalion."

It seemed that those in the battalion who were not on the front line, those that were in the vicinity of the enclosure when this was going on, were surrounding the jeep.

Colonel Hadi sensing an embarrassing scene with battle-weary warriors thought it better not to follow through with the arrest. "This is not the time or place to continue this discussion. We're in the centre of a major theatre of war and must continue to fight for our beloved President."

He looked at the two party members. "Gentleman, this situation shall be resolved in due course, and I will contact you when I have reviewed the situation." He paused. "Please, Mr Shariq and Mr Zaman, let us return to the office." He saluted Lieutenant Jawaarl and the three men got into the jeep and disappeared in the opposite direction of the front.

Jawaarl looked at Safiya. "Doctor Mahdi, please excuse these idiots. I will write my report and have Captain Fayed counter sign it. If you remember, he was the officer who accompanied you earlier."

Safiya forced a half smile, and just as she went to turn away, a car pulled up with Fayed at the wheel. He got out and addressed those who remained outside the enclosure, "I would like to report that Lieutenant Bakir, the officer shot earlier this morning, is comfortable in the field hospital and is expected to make a full recovery thanks to the work carried out by Dr Mahdi." And just like that, Safiya's smile was no longer forced.

Fayed then saluted Jawaarl, returned to his truck, and drove off towards the dug outs on the front line. And the small crowd that had gathered to support Safiya before the arrest, gradually went about their business.

The noise of war continued to rage around her, she seemed now immune and this showed with the smile on her face. Moments later, she got a lift back to the field headquarters, and then back to Baghdad.

*****

This incident was not forgotten, however, and the incident involving the party member and his alleged charges came back to trouble Safiya. A few weeks later the status of her arrest was reported back to the headquarters of the Ba'ath party and a review was carried out.

It was the party members' joint decision to make an example of anyone that showed an unwillingness to support the President's orders, that is to lay down your life for our beloved country

After the hearing Safiya shrugged, she knew in herself if she had her way, then every young wounded soldier would be sent home to recuperate. She was a doctor not a politician.

Her attitude was considered to be weak by the Ba'ath party, and a joint hearing between the army and the Ba'ath party was to take place in the Basra barracks in four weeks' time and she was to remain under house arrest until then.

Her charge was for 'overstepping a doctor's responsibilities', and the charge was in relation to 'sending fit soldiers home for recuperation when they were needed on the front line'.

Chapter 26

A Language for Every Season

Spring 1986

Jenny Jocyline was a tall, leggy, American-Jewish girl from the state of Virginia. She had a short, blond, chic hairstyle, she wore no make-up and her light-blue eyes emphasised her well-shaped but small facial features.

She walked smoothly and confidently, and her poise could have been that of a model on the catwalk. Jocyline finished the first part of her higher education in the US, where she graduated with a degree in business studies at Virginia University. She then applied and was accepted by the New Sorbonne University in Paris, and four years later, graduated in Arabic and Modern Hebrew.

Soon after, she applied and was accepted for a job at the American Embassy. When her security clearances were authorised, she began to become involved in more classified projects, as her seniors thought her ideal for this type of work. Even though they carried out a series of trials and confidential checks on her, she never faltered. It wasn't long before the Central Intelligence Agency approached her and suggested that she take more of an interest in international affairs.

One year later, she had a new vocation and was a fully-fledged agent working for the United States government.

Most of the action was now happening in the Middle East and, with her language skills, she did not go amiss with her seniors and they immersed her in more serious duties. Her first posting was working at the American consulate in Jordan, and after two years of carrying out minor duties, she was transferred to Dubai, a civilised and rich, but congested, emirate. It was an ideal place to conduct international business meetings as it was a beautiful city, while also being the centre of international intrigue.

She was a natural when infiltrating groups of random people, she easily joined casual conversation, with her soft Virginian accent not raising suspicions in any sector of the populace. She had the ability to glean the right intelligence from the most casual conversations.

An attractive girl was a direct challenge for the wealthy Arabs that frequented the hotels in Dubai, and her presence soon attracted other nationalities. One country in particular were checking her past, with an emphasis on ancestry. The Israelis, who are always looking to strengthen their intelligence, passed her file onto Mossad. They were already tailing her and ready to talk business when the appropriate time arrived.

On one particular day, in the early afternoon, Jenny returned to her hotel close to Jumeirah island. She was listening to passing strangers, evaluating what was said, finding out what they did and what they were really up to.

Caesars Palace, her hotel, was only a temporary home. She only intended to remain in this accommodation until other suitable housing could be found.

She started heading for the hotel swimming pools, she did not care which one, as long as she had peace and the facility to order drinks.

It was time to have a break from other people's bullshit, so in a peaceful mindset, she collected a towel from the kiosk and left her valuables in the safe deposit box before making her way down to the pool that was the least busy.

She had not noticed the man shadowing her, and he continued undetected as she settled down under the shade of a canopy.

There were two sunbeds in close vicinity, so she positioned her towel and reading material on one and started to prepare to sit on the other. The shadow appeared and pretended to look for something on the floor under the pretence that he had lost his vanity ring.

Jocyline looked up, annoyed. She was suspicious that someone had taken away her privacy so quickly.

But she joined in the game she thought he was playing, perhaps it would amuse her rather than cause her stress. As she tried to feign naivety and help this man look for his imagined ring, she changed her opinion of him. He seemed charming and was particularly attractive, so she let her guard down slightly.

"Did you say you've mislaid a ring? Perhaps you should ask the concierge, if you haven't already."

"It was nice piece, but it's of little value and it's not sentimental." He laughed.

She relaxed, smiled, and asked him what nationality he was.

"I'm an Israeli," he shrugged and then added, "you know, from Tel Aviv."

"OK, I thought I recognised your accent. I'm from Richmond, Virginia. My name is Jenny."

"That's a beautiful name, it rolls off the tongue, and the state of Virginia is so full of history and originality."

She did not mention her heritage, although he may have guessed. She decided she liked this muscular and charming man.

"I go by the name of Criff, but you can call me what you like."

She knew whatever he told her may not be the truth, especially what he did for a living, nevertheless she would ask.

"What do you do for a living, Mr Criff?"

"Just Criff."

"You told me to call you what I liked."

"OK, OK," he laughed. "I work for the Israeli Consulate."

"You mean Mossad?" She was bold.

"I said the consulate."

"What do you want from me, Mr Criff?"

"I'm aware of your heritage and we would like you to work for us… on a part-time basis."

"I can't, I've sworn allegiance to the United States."

"That is very honourable for you to say so, but our race is related to yours and it needs protection. As we are allies, we must stick together. I understand your allegiance, but we need you… and nobody needs to know."

"You're asking me to be a traitor and spy against my own country, that's treasonable, Mr Criff."

"Jenny, look, all we need to know are the risks to our mother country, and we'll require you to inform us regarding any dangers that might be forthcoming, is that treasonable?"

"Anything that I find out must go through my superiors first, otherwise I become a double agent."

"If the Iraqis develop or obtain nuclear warheads, they have the range to reach our country. Our very existence is in jeopardy, and I expect a warning from someone with the same heritage. After all, we're all expected to be partners in such a situation."

Jocyline remained silent whilst Criff collected his belongings from the floor where he had left them when he arrived.

"If I learn anything that puts our country in danger, I'll let you know. So please send me a direct number I can use to contact you at any time, you understand what I'm saying?"

"Yes, I will contact you soon."

Without a smile, or any recognition of his success, he somehow faded into the background.

Chapter 27

Like a Bad Penny

Spring 1986 dispirited

Copping was feeling downhearted, he thought the situation with Safiya was going to have put him in a bad place with Mahmoud and the team. He had broken the sacred code that separated foreigners from the locals and he wasn't looking forward to facing Mahmoud and the team.

The more he turned the situation around in his head, the more he was convinced that they may rescind his visa. After all, most of the serious work was now complete and they no longer needed him. But his projects had been successful, and he could only hope that this would be his saving grace.

He may, of course, be given the alternative of marriage. However, while marrying Safiya would maintain her honour, it would tie him to Iraq for a very long time as he would be required to pay for her education, and that was a daunting thought.

He wanted to continue their friendship, she seemed so driven yet so lonely. But he found it difficult to imagine a future with her, their lives were too far apart.

Then the telephone rang, it was O'Byrne. He wanted to talk and was waiting downstairs.

*****

"You know, Copping, I haven't bothered you at all since you arrived and you should be happy, but instead you come down to see me and you look like the most miserable man on earth. What's the matter?"

"What can I do for you, Mr O'Byrne?"

"First, you can tell me what is making you feel this way, perhaps I can help?"

"I had a friend visit me in my room, she was a lady, an Iraqi, and a medical doctor."

"And you were caught red-handed?"

Copping did not reply but then asked, "Again, what do you want, Mr O'Byrne?"

"Look, Copping, you already know how much my superiors and I have helped you. We've made you very comfortable here in Iraq. I've arranged your work and covered your illegal past, then you reward yourself with females, the very evil I told you to stay away from, and now this!"

"Mr O'Byrne, I know you've helped me out on many occasions, but then I've helped you too. What about the information I've provided since I arrived? Your seniors must had found some of it interesting!"

"That's codswallop. You were horny, and you wanted to have your way with her." He paused and glared at Copping. "You're so naïve! It's been two minutes and you're already filling your boots. May I remind you that you're working in a Muslim country as a guest. You shouldn't be frolicking with anyone, at any time, especially with those who are not easily replaced when the country is at a war." O'Byrne drained some of the beer he had been nursing since Copping arrived.

"I know, and I'll face the consequences tomorrow." Copping was miserable.

"Apart from that, my dear boy, I require some detailed information from you as soon as possible. You may not have much time, but I'm relying on it."

Copping sighed, "What do they want to know so urgently?"

"They want to know what progress Saddam has made on his nuclear program. Have they ordered uranium or not? And if they have, we want to know the progress on their processing facility. If they've received material, where is it stored? Also, my bonny lad, find out what quantities of oil have been exported this year, and what the plans are for next year." O'Byrne paused to look around, ensuring their conversation was still private.

"They want to know the Iraqis' oil export schedule, and their target price. If they sell low, as he might do in order to support his war effort, then this will affect the Russian economy." His eyes scanned the room again as he took a swig of his drink. "And one more thing, we're aware that the Iranian forces are doing remarkable things in the war, but their country should be virtually bankrupt after their civil war, so tell me who is supporting them financially, someone must be and in a big way."

Copping needed to think quickly enough to keep O'Byrne off his back, he must give him something otherwise he might just pull the plug on him altogether.

"Well, Copping," continued O'Byrne, "you've been in Baghdad now for some considerable time, I know that you have influential contacts and I'm sure you've learnt a lot, but now I've come to collect. I want answers to my questions, so please, get out there and find them, quickly."

He finished his drink, stood up and without looking at Copping again, walked away and out through the hotel's rotating doors.

Spring 1986

Copping was waiting for the staff bus and when it arrived, it was half full as usual. As he got on, he smiled and said, *"Sabaah altishayr"* (*"*Good morning*"*). Copping had been told not to greet women directly, and most passengers were usually women, so only some responded, while the more traditional ladies kept their faces averted and their eyes fixed on something out of the window.

The morning trips were always a happier time, as in the evening it was common to look out of the bus and see cars that had coffins strapped to the roof, with the relatives or friends of the deceased inside the vehicle suffering with immense grief. Copping found that, in general, the Iraqi people were good and kind folks, but the country was at war and most had suffered a personal loss, and their mood would often reflect this. In conversation, the local people were embarrassed and ashamed to be involved in a war with so much horror and loss of life, especially when none of them knew or understood the cause of it.

Watching the institute workers on the bus was upsetting, seeing so many young people going to work in such beautiful weather. Their faces were all beaten down and haggard, they had nothing to look forward to in their forthcoming days, only hardship and grief.

*****

Copping felt that he had served O'Byrne well, he had met the right people through the tennis club that he formed for this purpose, and had gathered notes by listening to the various strains of business visitors that passed through. These lists would often include their reasons for travelling to Baghdad. He had submitted long lists of personal details: names, contact numbers, and the details of business deals made on their visits.

He had full control of the construction of the pipeline and could accelerate or slow the progress, depending on what O'Byrne wanted. Any delay to the completion date might cause him a problem, but he would overcome this when and if it was necessary, it was more important to keep O'Byrne happy.

However, because Copping had retained some important pieces of information, if any of it were to be leaked, the suspicion would almost certainly fall on him.

He assumed that O'Byrne would not know about Yellow Cake uranium or the connection with Niger, nor would he know about the special storage facility associated with Project 109, and Copping was not about to tell him.

He had already given O'Byrne information regarding Iraq's change in weaponry, in which they upgraded their scud B missiles from a 300 to a 500-mile radius.

Chapter 28

Making Contact with a Friend

Copping had not seen or heard from Safiya for some time and was beginning to worry for her safety, but he could not contact her as he knew their phones would be tapped. And any connections with Leila might have similar consequences, because although her ethnic background would not draw the same attention, it might reflect on him for other, more immoral, reasons.

He thought deeply on his complex situation, he knew it was paramount to maintain a low profile and stay out of anything that may cause problems with either the Iraqi regime, or O'Byrne.

*****

The construction progress for work on the underground storage bunker had slipped and this was causing Copping to have sleepless nights. He needed to look at different methods on how to get it back on track before Mahmoud noticed that there was little leeway between the forecast date and the promised date.

Copping's laborious trip to the office the next day seemed to take much longer then in the past and he became irritated. It was not only the longest, but it was probably the worst bus in the fleet. It was noisy, bumpy, and slow.

Disembarking, he wearily headed upstairs, his mind still in turmoil, and began to wander what was the next catastrophe that would befall him. Then, reaching his office, he was surprised that Sadr greeted him warmly.

"*Sabaah altishayr,*" Copping spoke first, and got a smile in return. "Do you want a coffee? Then we can sit down and talk."

Sadr looked at him, and Copping thought he showed a smile, "And what is this I hear about your new Iraqi friend?"

Copping was expecting this and nodded and wearily, sitting down before he answered.

"Yes, I was caught with a woman," he replied. "But as I told Jamal, the party interrogator, she's a close friend."

Sadr smiled, lent forward on his elbows, and in a low voice said, "That's life, my friend." He sighed. "I qualified here in Iraq for my first degree, then moved to Moscow for my second. We were only given one year to get up to speed with the language, as the engineering course was in Russian, but during the next year I rarely went to my language classes and my attendance marks were very low. And yet, after the year, I spoke the language like a native and passed the oral test with the highest marks in the class. And do you know why?"

He looked at Copping, who was still trying to assess his meaning.

"Tell me, Sadr."

"Because I got myself a girlfriend and learnt the language between the sheets," answered Sadr, with a wide grin.

Ed smiled, finally catching on.

"I passed with nearly with a mark of 90%, and I might add that I was also told the same as you, from a political party much stronger than the one here. The Russians also kept a 'strictly do not talk or mix with locals' regulation, and were expected to comply." He laughed. "It turned out OK though, I never spied on anyone, nor did I dissent Russian politics."

He paused, still resting on his elbows, and said softly, "Look, my friend, I am a senior Ba'ath party member and quite honestly I'm not interested if you fuck all the girls in Baghdad. But please, these things must be kept a secret, don't invite trouble."

He got up and walked over to the coffee table. "Another coffee, Edward?"

Later that day.

In the evening Copping ordered room service, choosing a stir fry for his main meal, and to spoil himself he ordered a bottle of Chablis, put his feet up on the settee, and watched CNN news until he went to bed at 10 o'clock.

Things had been quiet over the past six weeks in Baghdad, and it seemed that the Iranians had given up attacking the capital directly and instead concentrated on more strategic targets, such as oil-fields and main highways.

But situations in war are never consistent as one would expect in life, and this particular night the Iranians chose to hit Baghdad using their new scud missiles purchased from North Korea. These had an improved range of 280–350 kilometres and the first of two that were dispatched that night hit very close to the east of the city, one landing close to the Sheraton Hotel.

Copping was asleep, but on impact the blast threw him out of bed. Completely dazed and trying to think what had happened he lay on the floor and methodically felt each of his limbs to make sure he was still in one piece.

Now quickly coming to his senses he pulled on shirt and trousers and made for the door, he would move along the corridor outside keeping his hands on the wall, this was following procedure, soon he reached the emergency exit stairs where he joined others making their way down the stairs. All looked in a dishevelled state, and this made Copping feel a whole lot better.

Outside the hotel there was complete pandemonium, with people shouting, some crying and a lot of flashing lights. He sat down on a concrete ledge and just stared straight ahead and he guessed he was in shock. It was only then a staff member alerted him to blood running down his arm.

He walked unsteadily to the foyer and reception area, and it seemed the whole hotel had assembled. Some were screaming, whilst others were groaning from the pain of their injuries. Copping had stumbled past two or three inert forms on the floor and felt guilty, as he did not offer to help them. If they were alive, it would be better if the medics attended to them. He thought it would be best if he got a taxi to the Irish hospital, they would not yet be involved and it would be better to be patched up by someone who can relate in English, he wanted to know how bad his injury was!

A few minutes later, he found a cab and was soon at the Irish hospital, and by this time blood had stemmed to a point.

He was still in shock, but somehow kept conscious and was soon knocking on the surgery door.

"Hello, Robert Maris here."

Copping explained the situation and added that he would prefer to stay out of the Iraqi medical system and asked the doctor if he could patch him up.

"Mr Copping, look, I'm an orthopaedic surgeon. I don't handle trauma or war wounds."

"Robert, you know how difficult it is for a foreigner to go through the local system." He recognised the doctor from one of the cricket matches.

The doctor seemed to recognise Copping too. "Okay, well it shouldn't be any different but look, if you can get down to our theatre where the conditions are sterile, then I'll take a look at it and see what can be done. The only other thing I can do is send you to a trauma specialist."

Chapter 29

A Popular Man

Summer 1986

Over the next few weeks, the Iranians bombed the city with their Korean-supplied scud R17's as they were now in a better position to attack from varied locations.

The hotels on the south side started to empty and Copping lost his information source. His connections had either moved away or decided not to visit Baghdad during the attack. He had not pursued his practice of calculating the missile drop areas and the new version of the scuds had more control and calculation of range, making them impossible to assess.

Tom Patten made a fleeting visit but when he witnessed the damage caused by the new missiles, he realised that staying in central hotels posed a high risk, forcing him to use his return ticket to London. However, before he left, Patten organised for Copping to move into a safe house.

Copping was disappointed not be living in the same luxury hotel that he had begun to think of as his home. He also dreaded this way of living: washing dishes, washing clothes, and cooking meals. He had grown accustomed to the special treatment at the hotel, and had forgotten what it was like to live independently, but he followed Patten's instructions and moved in.

The property was leased by another division of the company and was used infrequently by the power plant service engineers. There were normally two of them that visited the house around four times a year, and when residing in the house they would travel to Mosul on a daily basis.

Although it was located in an area that was considered safe, Copping found the place inconvenient for his own private operations. One annoying factor was the surrounding desert, as the winds would pick up the sand and scatter it over everything inside and outside of the house.

The house had four bedrooms and Copping picked the largest, which was positioned on the ground floor at the rear of the house. Soon after he moved in, he made a point of scrupulously cleaning the place, but soon found this was required as a daily a chore, one that he was not prepared to do. And the chances of hiring help were low due to the location of the house and its vicinity to the war.

Long after the interactive club games finished, Copping found it difficult to sustain the intelligence trail that he had been feeding to O'Byrne, mainly due being so disconnected from people. He rarely went out during the week, and even if he did, his activities such as the tennis bookings and general bar discussions no longer existed.

Copping found this mode of living to be very lonely, spending every night in the house alone. It was a chore to go to town, and he was worried that the lack of information for O'Byrne could cause him trouble. He would need to get back to the hotel and his previous life as soon as possible.

His method of transport to work had also changed, as he now used the car to drive into town and park at the Sheraton, before joining the staff bus.

One Thursday, Copping was on his way back from work, only having had a half day, and dropped his car off at the Sheraton to have a drink with his old friend JP. Although he had not seen him for a few weeks, Copping was not surprised when he saw JP sitting in his regular spot at the bar. It was as though he had not moved since last time he saw him, always watching and listening. Nevertheless, it was great to be in his friend's calm presence and revel in his enthusiasm for life.

"It's great to see you, Ed. When will you move back? Things are normal here again and besides, I miss you."

"Now that I'm in this bar, I want to be back sooner rather than later. I'll discuss this matter with Patten on Monday, when he gets back into the office."

"Oh, by the way there are a few messages for you at reception, the receptionist has been asking after you. So, I suggest you go collect, there may some juicy information to read."

Half an hour later.

Copping returned with a small bundle of envelopes, and carefully opened each one, scanning the contents without saying much, to the annoyance of JP. The last envelope was the most interesting, and after reading its contents he shrugged and turned to JP, who by this time was pretending to read his book.

"Well, I have been out of the loop these past few weeks and it seems my friend Safiya has been panicking, with no answer to her three notes."

"Well, are you going to reply?" JP asked.

"I will but I ought to arrange to see her after I move back in here."

"Nonsense, your house is the best place. Nobody sees you, just think of what you can get up too!"

"Please, JP, behave yourself."

"Go, it's the weekend! Now hurry up and phone her."

Copping walked over to the receptionist and asked to use the phone booth, and after a few seconds, he was connected.

Because of any line bugging that the secret police may have arranged, he was careful to leave a coded sign she would understand to call him back.

A few minutes later his telephone rang!

"Safiya, is that you?"

"Yes, where have you been? I've missed you."

"Because of the situation, my company moved me into a safe house."

"A house, by yourself?"

"With two others, but they aren't in the house very often." He paused. "Most of the time I have it to myself."

"How long will you stay there, Edward?"

"Not long I hope, I want to come back to the Sheraton, the house is too dusty."

"That's Baghdad, always full of dust."

There was a pause, then Safiya broke the silence.

"What are you doing today? Perhaps we can get together, or maybe tomorrow as I'm free."

"That would be nice, where can I pick you up?"

"You know, it's difficult for me to be seen on the streets alone, especially if the wrong people see me getting into your car."

"Well, Safiya, where and when?"

"Give me the address of your house and please make sure the door is open for me, as I will come by taxi, and will wear a head-scarf. Normally I use the same driver when I go to the hospital, so it won't draw attention, and he's a good man."

Copping gave her the address, then returned to the bar and said goodbye to JP.

"Are you on a promise, Edward?"

"I shouldn't have told you anything, JP. You'll tell the world my intentions, so if anyone wants to know, I'll be at home. Alone."

"Pull the other one old boy," JP laughed.

"I'll be back in the hotel soon, JP, and we can get back to normal."

An hour and a half later.

Copping was feeling apprehensive; he had already been sitting in the house for an hour. However, he had no reason to worry as a moment later the large door swung open and Safiya, looking absolutely radiant, with a smile on her face, walked towards him.

She wore a long, blue headscarf that covered her head and shoulders, although it looked large enough to cover the whole of her body. In a minute she was in front of him, he gently lifted her scarf and kissed her on both cheeks, as the soft black curls of her hair dropped to just above her shoulders. She wore a white blouse and tight black trousers, her shoes looked like a standard hospital issue, flat soles with lace ups, but she looked beautiful in the simplest of clothing.

"Edward, I'm sorry I'm late but the driver found it difficult to find the road. He said this was a new street, and the houses are so large, he thought this house belonged to three generations of an Iraqi family."

"I must apologise for the dust, Safiya, it's not my house and believe me, it will be better once I move back into the hotel."

She smiled and after searching through her bag, took out a cigarette. When, looking across at him, and not receiving a rebuff, she continued to light it.

Taking a few puffs, she slowly walked around the room, asking Copping questions as she did. "What have you been doing since we last met? Did I get you into trouble with the authorities over our meeting?"

"Yes, I did get a tough talking to in the hotel but at the office, Sadr, my party shadow, told me in these circumstances it must be a secret. He told me his own story from when he was studying in Russia. He explained that he was given a year to learn the language, and he spoke and read perfectly when it came to his exam."

Copping was smiling at the memory of the story. "He said he only attended two language sessions during the year, but still finished with the highest marks in the class because he had a girlfriend and was 'learning the language between the sheets.'"

Safiya smiled. "That I can understand." Then her smile quickly disappeared. "But do not trust him, I have checked up on all of those involved in splitting us up at the hotel, and he may be the one that was responsible for alerting the guard."

"That's surprising, he seems a fair man to me." He looked to her for further response, but she continued circling the room puffing on her cigarette. When she had finished, she walked over to Copping, who was now sitting on one of the chairs at the dining table.

When she came to his chair, she stopped, put her hand around his neck and slowly sat down on his lap.

"I hate this war and the people who are running our country, they're deplorable, ruthless and controlling." She still had not mentioned her recent ordeal and had no inclination to do so, she thought it would be too much of a distraction, especially as she was waiting her hearing and still under house arrest.

Copping did not know what to say and remained silent.

"Oh Edward, you don't know half of the problems with the authorities that I have to go through." She then pulled his head towards hers and kissed him softly on his lips, but as he started to respond, she held him back.

"Not here Edward, let's go somewhere more suitable."

She slid from his lap, and he gestured towards the back of the house where the door to his bedroom was open. Soon they were both on top of the bed, undressing each other and laughing loudly. Both were happy and enjoying the moment, but to choose who was enjoying the time more it was Safyer, because for a short time she was free she intended to make the most of it as tomorrow may never come.

It wasn't long before they were entwined, totally together, enjoying every emotion. They were both hungry for each other, but Safiya soon laid back on her pillow, relaxed and happy.

"Edward," she whispered, with her eyes closed. "I must get out of the country, Iraq will always will be my home, but I must go and live a free life."

She paused for some time and then murmured, just loud enough for Copping to hear, "You must come with me, please Edward, in a few hours we could be in Damascus."

She slipped from the bed and stood upright, wearing nothing except her underwear. It was then that he noticed her full figure was ash white, and he realised it would not be the custom for an Arab girl's body to see the sun.

Waiting for his response, she reached for her handbag and pulled out a cigarette pack, but before she could put it to her lips, he was close. He slipped his hand behind her back and unclipped her bra. He then took her cigarette out of her hand, put it on the side and pulled her onto the bed. It was the start of a wonderful weekend in a house that, until this moment, he had hated.

Saturday evening.

Safiya walked from the house, dressed in the large headscarf that she held at her neck, with the head section pulled over her face.

Leaving this way, no one was to know who she was or where she had been, except from the driver whom she trusted. After walking twenty yards down the road, she turned left and got into his taxi.

He did not say a word on the drive back to her lodgings. It seemed he was trying to come to terms with a doctor staying in a strange neighbourhood for more than a day, or perhaps was he deliberating how much he could get for delivering this information to a party member?

Copping still did not have the slightest inkling regarding Safiya's intolerable experience, or the culpability she faced regarding the charges made by the Ba'ath war committee.

Chapter 30

Jocyline Makes a Show

Summer 1986

In Baghdad the bombing had ceased, the Iranians had changed tactics and were now concentrating on military targets in the south. When the attacks decreased, businesspeople returned to the city and the hotels were once again in full operation.

A constant stream of visitors continued to arrive in Baghdad and this remained constant throughout the next few months.

Copping was meeting most of them one way or another, and although he had moved from the Sheraton to the house, he was still the keeper of the tennis reservation book. He had found a way to persuade Patten that it was best if he stayed at the hotel at weekends and moved back to the house during the week.

His close friendship with JP, meant the weekends were spent sharing many pleasurable evenings with him and friends at the either of the two local hotels.

On one occasion, a tall, rangy man entered the bar and both Copping and JP recognised his American accent. Like most New Yorkers, he showed off his confident and extroverted traits when, without an introduction, he asked Copping and JP if they would join him, subsequently buying them a drink in the process.

It wasn't long before he was telling them his life story, his successes, and his failures in business. In a short time, they had found out his age, his wife's name, his business and the reasons he was in Baghdad. He was vice-president of a company that specialised in ocean pipe-laying, and was in Baghdad to lease Iraq a number of lay-barges, but the recent attacks by the Iranians had delayed the confirmation of the contract.

The New Yorker, Laurence Moore, was an intellectual with a very wealthy family. He was married to a beautiful, intelligent American woman, and much to the annoyance of Copping and JP, he assured them that they would never be given the chance to meet her. Though he did not say why, they both made the assumption was that he thought that they were both a pair of bar huggers.

But Moore did not waste time when it came to meeting new people. Since arriving from the States only two nights earlier, he had already struck up a friendship with an American girl called Jenny Jocyline. He went on to tell them that she was living in the Hotel Melia on the other side of the river, and would be there for some time, as though he was implying that they should meet her. It soon became apparent this lady was lonely and wanted to meet other nice people, so Moore suggested that she join a tennis tournament at one of the hotels.

Copping remained quiet and decided not to intervene, he was forever wary, and could not forget O'Byrne's warning regarding females being the biggest danger. But JP would not let his pal off the hook and went on to explain Copping's involvement in organising tennis at the Meridian. He even suggested, to Copping's annoyance, that he would fix Jocyline up with a playing partner.

As the drink flowed, Moore became more cordial, and the story of his life started to unfold, a story that hooked his two listeners.

Moore was a handsome man of about forty years of age, he was also very tall and as a consequence had a slight stoop. His ability to talk about nearly every subject under the sun kept those listening engrossed. He was a captivating storyteller, though his eyes did most of the talking, and JP and Copping hung onto every detail as he rattled on about his family and lifetime achievements.

It was good entertainment, but both were relieved when he stopped to take a sip from a large whisky he had ordered at the start of their conversation.

They had not said a word during this time and were both glad when he departed. He shook both of their hands whilst saying goodbye, left the bar, and passed through the hotel swing-doors, into the night.

Another man, who had partially interacted during the conversation with Moore, made an obvious observation. "Some of these guys can tell a tale, can't they?"

Both Copping and JP nodded and introduced themselves. "This is our local, so we're used to hearing everyone's life story, but anyway, are you staying in this hotel?" asked JP.

"Yes, I'll be staying here over the next six months or so. We'll probably see each other a lot over that time, that is if you guys are up for it."

"We will," answered Copping. "Are you here on business?"

"Yes, I work for BAC as a missile and defence systems analyst. We're based in the UK but I've worked out of Dubai for the past two years."

"What did you say your name was?"

"Oh, my name's Mornington Ryder. Quite a mouthful, I know, but the name comes from my father."

"Wow. Yes, it is quite a mouthful. But please join us, I'm sure we'll cross paths in the near future anyway."

Copping felt comfortable in Ryder's company, although the main attraction was that he might learn something about missiles.

A few days later.

Copping came home from work and was surprised to see Moore in the lobby. He was in the company of a very tall, slim woman, who had short hair that framed her face and figure. As he got closer to her, he noticed her eyes were a bright blue. He also noticed that she was quite indifferent to her surroundings, as she ignored Moore and gazed into in the distance. Moore greeted Copping warmly and both were acting as if they were long lost friends instead of two guys who had drunk together in the bar only two days prior.

Moore turned to the lady and introduced her as Jenny Jocyline, the American from Virginia. She shook Copping's hand with a light grip, but did not release his hand immediately. Instead, she watched Copping's reaction for a few seconds before releasing it.

"How long have you been in Baghdad?" asked Copping, transfixed by her confidence and beauty.

Before she could answer, Moore interrupted. "Look, guys, I have to fly to Abu Dhabi in an hour and a half, so I'll leave you two to discuss tennis and the history of Virginia."

"OK, give me call when you return," said Copping, reassuring Moore of their fast friendship. Moore shook Copping's hand, kissed Jocyline on both cheeks, turned, and disappeared through the revolving doors of the hotel.

"Well, it's always nice walking in from work with nothing planned, only to be introduced to a beautiful American lady."

"It's nice for me too, Edward. I'm glad to have met you." She smiled and asked, "What brings you to Baghdad?"

"I work for an international oil services company, and we're contracted out to the Iraqi petroleum company. What about you?" He was more interested in what she did.

"Oh, I work for the American Embassy, I recently transferred from Dubai."

"What do you do at the embassy, Jenny?"

"Consular work, you know, American people abroad, that sort of thing."

Copping looked at his watch. "Look, I'd love to chat now but I have to get up to my room, I've still got some business with the London office. Perhaps we can meet later, some dinner here or at your hotel?"

"That would be nice."

"OK, I'll come over to your hotel."

"No, please Edward. I'll come here, it suits me better, shall we say seven o'clock?"

Four weeks later.

Following their first meeting, Jocyline and Copping had met on three occasions and had been getting on well. However, the last time they met, she had reacted strangely, and her behaviour had disturbed him.

Although their dates were becoming more intimate, he felt that it was time to end their friendship, he thought it was unfair on Safiya. But then something extraordinary happened when they met for drinks in his room. She was sitting opposite his desk, when suddenly she got up and hurled herself across the room, landing on him with her legs astride his. It was quite astonishing, and completely out of character.

He thought it was a joke and they both laughed, but it seemed a game to her and she teased him, "Let's kiss". Although he was aroused, he put his hands around her waist to stop her from proceeding any further, and she moved quickly away, returning to the chair. He was still so surprised that it had happened and the whole situation made him very uncomfortable, it was if she was playing with him.

"What was that all about?" asked Copping in surprise.

"I just remembered that you told me that you had a girlfriend here in Iraq, and you don't want to double dip, do you, Edward?"

"I did also tell you that I haven't spoken with her for some weeks. She's not actually a girlfriend." He could feel himself betraying Safiya as he spoke.

"Anyway Edward, I must go. We have a photo shoot at the Embassy, so I'll see you in the week, but give me a call at work."

Jocyline picked up her shawl and glided elegantly from his room, letting the door fall shut behind her.

Bemused by her antics, he shrugged, and without a further thought, he headed out to get a taxi and made for the British club. Perhaps he could forget about the unusual evening by spending some time with Leila.

However, he was disappointed as the only bar with life was the public section and a darts match was on.

As he was about to leave, he saw Richard and asked after Leila.

"She's been poorly but she's been asking about you." He was about to say something else, but then he seemed to think better of it and changed the topic of conversation. "By the way, Ed, do you still travel to Basra? 'Cause if you do, she wants a ride some time."

"That would make some good reading, Rich," Copping replied sarcastically. "Irishman working for the Iraqi government stopped whilst travelling to Basra with his Kurdish girlfriend!"

"Would that matter? If I tell her no, she'll be so disappointed."

"Sorry, Rich, it's not more than my life is worth, especially with the recent chemical attack at Falluja."

"OK, I'll tell her." He sighed, then added, "She'll be sorry she missed you."

Copping wandered about the club for an hour, then decided to head back to the hotel.

It was still early, but JP had already turned up for his nightcap when Copping arrived at around seven.

The lobby was crowded as two European flights had arrived and the first thing most of the passengers did when they arrived at the hotel was to have a beer at the bar and then get their name on the tennis reservations.

"Hi Ed, how are you?" A familiar voice came from across the bar. "Still looking after tennis? I could do with a game, anything to keep me fit."

"Nice to see you too, Mornington, and yes, I'm still looking after the court. I'm working on a few other things at the moment, but I'll see what I can do."

Mornington Ryder was going nowhere, it seemed he was in for the long shift in Iraq. This was good news for Copping, as he was still especially interested in him because of his work with missiles.

Ryder was a very big man, well over two metres tall, with a huge frame. Although he was a Scotsman by birth, he then moved to the south east of England and worked for BAC as a missile expert. Now in his late forties, he was always friendly and very talkative, the sign of a great salesman. Nevertheless, he never hung around too long or spoiled anyone else's company, nor did he talk about work, religion or politics. He did, however, like local scandal and whenever there were rumours, he was the man to disclose all of the theories.

"As a matter of fact, Ed, I saw you with a girl, Jenny, a few weeks ago. I knew her from my days in Dubai, but I couldn't stop to say hello as I was returning to the UK."

"You knew her before?"

"Well yes, I worked with her company many times, she's quite a woman!"

"Quite a woman?" Copping quizzed him.

"You may not want to know this, but I'm speaking as a friend here, she had a different man on her arm every time that I saw her. And these guys were not ordinary, you know, Sheiks and politicians, she could certainly pull the important guys."

"Are you sure the lady we're talking about is the one you knew?"

"Absolutely, after I left last time, she was going out with a colleague of mine. In fact, it was so serious that she told me they were to get married. But it's none of my business, and this guy was already married, so I don't know what that was all about."

In the short time that Copping had known Jocyline, he had liked her and did not want to pursue this type of dialogue, it was becoming too personal. However, Ryder had alerted him to the fact she was mixing with important Arabs, which was particularly interesting given her role as a Jewish Consulate official working in the American Embassy.

"Are you here closing some sort of deal Mornington, or is this a sales trip?" Copping tried to steer the topic away from Jocyline.

"I'm confirming a big deal, but I may have to stay in Baghdad to supervise the selection of our team of technicians."

"Are these missiles capable of a nuclear warhead?" Copping asked.

"They are, but you need a warhead first, which they haven't got at the moment. But still, these are some serious flying machines. These missiles go by the name of HWASONG-5's and they have a range of 600 kilometres. I'm just here to work on the control systems." Ryder took a large sip of his drink.

"And when will these scuds be available?"

"Now, now, Ed. I don't want to be giving out too much information, and I'm feeling quite tired, so I must go." He drained the last of his drink. "See you around."

Chapter 31

Life Goes on in London

Summer 1986

Tom Patten was a busy man and on his return to London, he needed to sort out some problems associated with the Iraqi pipeline contract, as it had been reported to him on his last day in Baghdad. There was a mismatch of pipework on one of the compressor stations at Umm Qasr and the piping needed a small redesign, according to Mahmoud there was utmost urgency in correcting the problem.

The initial engineering work and drafting could be done in the office, but the engineer would need to visit the site in order to assess the 'as built' sections of the plant involved.

Patten was agitated by the extra cost of what he deemed to be unnecessary work. It was apparent that the acceleration imposed by the command council had caused the problem and he felt the cost should be paid by the Iraqis, but under the circumstances he was not prepared to argue the difference. After all, it was only a small part of a huge overall contract price.

Then the telephone rang and disturbed his train of thought.

"Hello, Mr Patten, Webster of the SIS here. You'll remember that we spoke some time back regarding the tracing of a certain individual we were interested in interviewing, with regard to his IRA terrorist activities?"

Patten screwed up his face trying to remember the conversation.

"I'm sorry, Mr Webster. Although I do remember you calling, I have done nothing in tracing your man." He felt annoyed with himself for forgetting this, as he was now aware of the importance of his caller.

"That's disappointing, Patten, but you may have some ideas, I assume?"

"We have a man working with us called Edward Copping, but this person is indisputably an honest and clever individual, who is an important part of the Iraqi team. I haven't a clue if he's your man or not."

"I think you've told me what I wanted to know, but I might warn you that we may want to extradite him to answer questions concerning his role within the IRA and his illegal activities since he has been on the run. Is that clear, Mr Patten?"

Patten felt agitated, the last thing he wanted was a further imbalance with the construction team in Iraq. The redesign was one thing, but the head of foreign affairs threatening him over an employee was something else.

Webster could do whatever he liked, he was a powerful man, although it would be a personal problem for Patten if he did carry out his threat and arrest Copping. He must find a way to stall Webster and give a little more time for Copping to finish the work on the south pipelines project. He also knew Copping was involved in other work and needed to be tactful.

"That's clear, Mr Webster, and I'm prepared to help, but not until the work that he's carrying out at the moment is finished. I suggest you call back in a few weeks and we can discuss it further."

"That sounds fair to me Patten, but I will be looking further into the matter, and in the meantime, I would be grateful if you kept me informed of the situation on a weekly basis."

"Absolutely, sir," Patten answered politely. After all, this man could give him trouble with his own board of directors.

One week later.

Steve Plant, the engineering draughtsman, was on his way to make design corrections to the large export pipework at the Umm Qasr site.

Plant was a tall, forty-year-old man. He was slim but had wide shoulders, his face was round, and his stubby nose pulled attention from the rest of his face. His long, black hair was swept back behind his ears, and when he was at work, he wore black horned-rimmed glasses.

He had worked in London most of his life, living with his wife and two children in the leafy village of Egham in the county of Surrey. His pastime was cricket and he was the star opening batsman for the local team.

Plant, however, was frustrated with his job as the travel to Iraq came at an in-opportune moment and he would miss the village's weekend cricket match.

The next morning, he arrived at Saddam Hussein airport, and was disappointed to be driven from the airport in a taxi, rather than a personal limousine, as the long journey that started in Heathrow began to take its toll.

The taxi dropped him off at the Petroleum Institute, and an Iraqi lady introduced herself, speaking slowly in broken English. "Please, Mr Plant, your bus is waiting to take you to the construction site in Az Zubayr. Your journey is expected to take approximately seven hours, however the bus is not full, so you will have plenty of space to spread out."

A bloody bus, is that all they could manage for a seven-hour journey? He thought to himself. He was missing his beloved cricket to travel on a bus that was taking him to a job he did not want to do. And things did not get much better during the next hour, as the bus was old and every bump jarred his body.

Once on the main thoroughfare, the surface was more consistent and he became comfortable enough to doze off. But this did not last long, and with each turn the bus hit another bump, wakening him, so he was forever changing position on the old double seat.

It seemed they had been driving for about four and a half hours, when suddenly he was jerked into an upright position. He was stunned by a thunderous noise, something that he never heard before, and he watched as the sky lit up, blinding him with a sudden brightness. It seemed as though the clouds were on fire. The bus rocked and the driver was struggling with his steering, he was swerving across the road, and the headlights from oncoming vehicles were disorientating him.

There was a blaring of horns, then more flashes and explosions. Now dizzy, the driver became unstable, and the bus suddenly swerved to the right, hitting a sand dune. There was a loud crashing sound, and then silence.

After what seemed like forever, the driver moved from his position at the wheel, shouted something in Arabic, opened the door and disappeared into the night.

Others in the bus ducked as they pushed their way down the aisle. Plant picked up his coat from the floor, where it had fallen before the accident, and followed the others down the bus and out of the emergency door on the side of the vehicle. Outside the atmosphere had changed, he now had to contend with sand and panic. People from the bus were screaming and running across the dunes randomly, and he had no choice but to follow them.

In the mayhem, he scrambled over soft dunes in an effort to catch up with the other passengers who were now well ahead of him. As he walked faster to try and approach them, another explosion went off somewhere close by. Plant felt the heat, stones, and dust hit him, and he fell down onto the sand, but still the explosions continued. The others from the bus seemed to have disappeared and he could only hear the noise of two or three females that were huddled and crying on the ground. He went to one of the ladies, she was holding an injured arm and he helped her to her feet. She shouted something in Arabic, holding his arm with one hand and pointing with the other in the direction of what Plant assumed was safety. He stumbled forward, still holding onto this woman, who he now noticed wore a long black dress and a black shawl over her head that kept falling around her shoulders as the moved forward.

Ahead of him were a few small buildings with one, maybe two, men standing by them and helping the others ahead of him. The other passengers were being directed towards one of the houses, and after he entered the same house, he dropped onto the floor in exhaustion and fear.

The bombs had finally stopped, and looking around saw he was in an open room. The woman he had helped had gone, hopefully directed to another house, so he put his head onto his forearm and closed his eyes.

The night turned out to be long and cold. Plant sat on the floor and hardly moved until a grey dawn arrived. He heard movement outside the hut but decided to stay put until those close to him in the room moved first. It wasn't long before he heard others moving around, they were speaking to each other in what seemed to be Hindu.

It was now light, and for the first time he saw his surroundings clearly, realising those around him were all from India. The smaller man of the four in the house turned and spoke to Plant. "This is terrible, we came here to work and have nearly been killed on the first day. We've travelled from Calcutta and arrived two days ago, we've not been able to wash or change our clothes since we left home." He stood up and stretched, then looked down at the Englishman. "Come, we must see what's going on, perhaps the company has sent a vehicle, and we can move from this area before the Iranians start shelling again."

The five of them walked from the house, while the sun tried to break through the grey sky above them. They walked along a section of the desert that was hardened from being trodden down by the local house dwellers, and Plant recognised some of the other passengers walking ahead of them. It seemed this was a deserted settlement, probably abandoned soon after the war started. He was informed by one of the men walking with him that this was an area on the road to Basra that was in range of the Iranian artillery.

After walking for an hour, the traffic started to increase and they held their hands in the air hoping someone would stop, but it seemed hopeless. The traffic was moving too fast, and the drivers probably thought it too dangerous.

But luck was on their side as an old bus, that was going much slower than the rest of the traffic, pulled into the area between the road and the desert.

"Where are you going?" asked Plant's new friend, he spoke to the driver in Hindi.

"I can take you to the Hotel Sheraton in Basra, but then you must find your own way from there as I have workman to pick up."

They drove slowly, the driver seemed to struggle with the controls but somehow kept it on the road. The truck's suspension was terrible and was jarring each time it went over uneven ground, causing a loud bang to go off each time.

During the five hours it took to hit the outskirts of Basra, they met plenty of military transport on the way, and it got worse as they drove through a built-up area close to the hotel.

The bus made two stops on the way and picked up a few people at designated places. Then, when they reached the hotel, Plant spoke with the receptionist and organised a small private bus to take them to the guest house near Az Zubayr. He had American dollars in his wallet and agreed a fee for the drive, explaining to the driver that their destination is a guest house that was situated on a defunct golf course.

The driver did not recognise the description that Plant explained to him, but once a defunct golf course was mentioned the driver knew exactly where to take them. There was no other golf course for a thousand miles.

*****

The roads were busy, and it took about forty minutes, with the driver stopping periodically to drop passengers off, but thankfully it was the end of a tumultuous journey for all those involved.

It had taken Plant nearly two days to travel from Baghdad airport to his accommodation and the work he was contracted to do had not even started. He intended to have a hot bath and sleep, and he felt that only then would he be ready to visit site.

But things went from bad to worse when he first saw the dilapidated guesthouse. He was bitterly disappointed with the location, and this became even more apparent when he entered the accommodation reception.

Inside the house, his stomach wrenched from the smell of raw fish drying on a clothes rail. He expected a luxury hotel, but had walked into a rat hole instead.

The man at the front desk said nothing and showed Plant his room, and when he entered, he slung his suitcase on the floor in disgust. He inspected the bed and then the shower, which were both in an abysmal state. The tiles were stained through age and filth, and some of them were even broken. The curtain hung from two hangers, and the shower head looked as if it had not been cleaned for years.

Now feeling hungry, he returned to the reception and asked the man on the desk if he could get some food, simultaneously using hand gestures to show what he meant. The receptionist shrugged and pointed to the watch on his hand, then lifted it up with one finger. Plant nodded and assumed the man meant that it would be one hour before food was served, but it could mean he would have to wait until one o'clock. Even so, he decided not to pursue the situation as he was tired, so returned to his room and decided to eat later.

Three hours later.

The site at Az Zubayr was well organised, with the office blocks set out in two lines of porta-cabins, all with power and air conditioning. Copping shared an office with two others from the same company, the construction manager, Graham Monk, and his assistant.

That day, both were out inspecting installations and left the office clear for Copping to brief the new designer, Steve Plant, when he arrived. He would also offer any advice before he met with the Iraqi client later in the week, then he could explain the redesign work he intended to do.

But it was now late afternoon and Plant had still not arrived. The situation was now becoming urgent, and Copping started to worry, so he decided to return to the office and see if any messages had arrived. During his walk he met a workman going the other way carrying a huge bundle.

Copping held his hand up and the man stopped, hoping he would be able to speak English.

"Sorry to stop you, but my name is Copping, and I work on site for the Petroleum Institute. Can you please tell me who you are?"

"Sorry mate, I'm just a lorry driver from the UK and I'm behind schedule." He looked as though he was trying to get away from Copping. "Look, I'm in a hurry, there's a huge back log of vehicles at the border and I'll never get home if I delay it any further. This bloody load on the waggon has been a bitch, there's no one on site to offload it and I'm really fed up." He sighed, then noticed Copping looking at the bundle he was carrying. "Oh, the box I understand contains documents for the London office, in case you need to know." His scouse accent was pronounced and he seemed to be an amenable guy.

"Who gave you the box to take back to the UK with you?"

"It's a favour for a guy called Ismail. You know, the graduate?"

"Yes, I do."

Copping approached the driver and said, "Mind if I take a look what my friend Ismail is sending back to the UK?"

"Not at all, mate, fill your boots. But don't take too long, I need to be on my way."

Copping cut the top carefully with his site knife and peered inside to see that the whole box was stuffed with plastic bags. He took off his glove to reach for one of the bags when the driver suddenly blurted.

"By the way, Mr Copping, when I left the offices there was a guy lying on the steps to your office. He was conscious but vomiting. He looked in a pretty bad state."

Copping suddenly started to panic, he was aware that no doctors were on site due to the holidays and this man would need help. He immediately stopped what he was doing, thanked the man, and hurried back to the office. He momentarily forgot about Ismail and the package.

A few minutes later, as he approached his office, he heard Plant before he could see him. He was lying on the three wooden steps that lead up to Copping's office, periodically heaving even though nothing was coming up. Copping turned him gently over, concerned that he was severely dehydrated.

"My name is Ed Copping, I take it you're Steve Plant?"

He nodded and Copping covered him with site coats, then poured him a glass of water, and placed a damp cloth on his head. He received a grateful moan from Plant as he did so.

"This is bollocks," groaned Plant. Who, while looking pale and dishevelled, started to explain his predicament.

He could not speak clearly because of his sickness, but Copping caught most of what he was saying, which sounded like a disastrous situation for a man coming into an unknown country.

"A bus?" Copping was astounded.

"Then the bus got bombed and I was lucky to get away with my life."

There was a pause and Copping waited for Plant to calm himself.

"The biggest load of bullshit is the bloody 'guest house'. Is that the best they can do?"

"Look, Steve, let us get you back to your bed and we can go from there."

Two hours later.

Plant lay in on his bed at the guest house and closed his eyes, he had stopped feeling nauseous and it seemed the sickness had gone. Copping wanted to get this man fit enough to complete the revised design, but at the moment it did not look like he would fully recover any time soon. So, Copping thought it would be best to let Patten know about the situation.

"Good evening Mr Patten, sorry to wake you up at home but we have a problem." He then proceeded to explain the situation.

"OK Ed, get him back on a plane, we don't want to have someone dying on us out there. In the meantime, I'll get a replacement ready."

During the time Plant was resuscitating, Copping started to remember the drug package and the possibility of fellow site members being involved in something illegal.

The sighting of Ismail driving along the Shatt-Al-Arab, his absence from sight without permission, the situation was now becoming clear, but he was not sure how to address this problem.

The following day.

Plant must have crossed his replacement in the air, as the new designer swiftly arrived at the airport and was expected to be at work the next day.

The replacement was a guy called Robert Norris. He was picked up in a car that was waiting for him at the airport, and whisked directly to the site in Az Zubayr without stopping for a break on the way.

Towards the end of the drive, Norris was desperate to relieve himself, and before the car had actually stopped, he had the door open and made a dash for the reception. At the last minute, he realised he would not make inside so diverted to the side of the guest house, and without a moment to spare he relieved himself against the outside wall. The driver, in the meantime, intent on practising his English, followed Norris and stood behind him as he gasped with relief. "I hoped you enjoyed the journey, sir. Should you need me to wait?"

Norris thought his English good enough to say, "I'm sorry I can't tip you now, but when you pick me up for the return, I will give you dinars."

The driver dropped his bag on the ground, returned to his car and drove off, disgusted that he was not acknowledged properly.

Chapter 32

Watch Out for Informers

Summer/Autumn 1986

It had been a difficult time for Copping and he thought that Mahmoud was starting to lose confidence in him. First the security people finding Safiya in his room, then the mess up with Plant, and now the suspicion that a Shia militia man was on the site.

What did the driver have in the bag that he was carrying for Ismail? Copping wondered. He would need to determine a strategy regarding his association with Ismail.

The irritation showed on his face as he checked into the Sheraton on Friday, he was looking forward to the weekend but not to his meeting with Mahmoud on the Sunday. He was a nice man, but he had a quick temper that often flared up when things went wrong. On a previous occasion, during a discussion in his office, Mahmoud jokingly pointed to a hook in the ceiling. Copping had seen these in many rooms whilst in Baghdad, but it was never made clear as to what they were used for, so Mahmoud explained.

"Mr Copping, if you look at the contraption in the ceiling," and he pointed to the hook, "please note that it is a memory of the 'old days'." Mahmoud gazed up at the hook. "When the secret police interrogated people, they hung them from these hooks." He looked back at Copping. "So far you haven't qualified to receive the same treatment, but there's still time."

Although they both laughed, Copping thought that Mahmoud's words could have been construed as threatening, and he shivered at the thought.

After bundling his dust-covered clothes into a hotel laundry bag, he hurried to the bathroom and ran a bath, soaking for as long as it took to forget the turmoil of Plant and the mystery of Ismail's package. He was convinced that his friend was involved in some sort of smuggling, and he assumed that it was drugs. But it was not the time to worry, he wanted to enjoy the weekend and put the recent incidents behind him until Sunday.

Leaning back against the cool slanting part of the bath, he slid down and let the warm water envelope his body. The scent of the bath salts allowed him to relax and he closed his eyes to enjoy the moment.

Copping must have fallen asleep as the telephone rang a long time before he picked it up, and he was still in a daze.

"Hi Ed, it's Jenny, I hope I find you well."

"Well, well, if it's not the love of my life, Jenny. How nice to hear from you, my girl."

"You never stop being the charmer, do you, Ed?" She giggled.

"Haven't seen you about recently Jenny, I started to think you had found someone else and got married." He thought about his discussion with Ryder, concerning her adventures in Dubai.

"Not yet, Ed, I'm still waiting for you," she teased. "But seriously, why don't you come over and visit me at the Melia, we can grab something to eat and catch up. I'm on the seventh floor, room 712."

"It might be a while. I fell asleep in the bath and was having an amazing dream, until you woke me."

"Poor you, but yes just put on a shirt and pants and come on over. I'll meet you either in the bar or in my room where I'll be getting ready."

"Can you give me an hour, Jenny? I'm knackered from travelling."

"OK, but if I'm not there come on up. I still have to take a shower, shampoo my hair, and make myself look good for you." She laughed.

"Sure, better that I escort you downstairs anyway, otherwise who knows what kind of attention you might get, all dressed up with nowhere to go."

"That'll do, Ed, I look forward to seeing you very soon."

After he put the phone down, he was rinsing off the bath suds in the shower and he began to wonder why she had called him in particular. She had so many male friends who seemed to be better suitors, which meant the call must be related to his job, so he must be careful.

Forty-five minutes later.

Copping arrived by taxi at the Mansour Melia on the banks of the Tigris, a huge block of a hotel, built only two years earlier. He felt very privileged as he sauntered up the steps to the main entrance, the door was held open by a fashionably dressed doorman.

He checked the bar quickly, but there was no sign of her, so he made for the lift and ascended to the seventh floor.

The door for room 712 was off the latch, so he gently pushed it open and called out, "Hi Jenny, it's me, Ed. Can I come in?"

She replied in an instant. "Come in, Ed, shut the door and come into the bathroom. You can help me with my hair.'

Her room was nicely furnished, although little smaller than his own, the furniture was of a better quality. She had an expensive-looking settee and a matching chair, the carpet was plush and the matching long curtains draped to the floor. She had papers scattered over the long coffee table.

The bathroom was on his immediate left, he could see straight into it, and his eye caught her almost naked body close to the sink. She was completely naked, except for a small underwear set, as she called him into the room.

"Oh Ed, please stop being so shy and come in and wash my hair, otherwise the soap will make my eyes red."

He walked towards her gingerly and took the shampoo from her hand, while she picked up the towel and covered her eyes.

His body was in close proximity to hers and it emphasised how slim she actually was against his own frame. He felt both aroused and terrified by the situation, and constantly kept a looking towards the adjoining room, in case she had someone waiting for him. She then bent over the sink, straightened her back and sighed. "Sorry, Ed, the strap of my bra is sticking into my back, would you undo it for me? It would be better if it was completely taken away."

He undid the hook and the bra fell to the floor. Copping was so distracted, he forgot that the shampoo was now under his arm, and it spilt onto her.

"Oh, come on Ed, you've split half the frigging bottle on the floor. Come on, let's get this done."

He then wet Jocyline's hair and applied the soap, rotating his hands slowly around her head, and as he did so his eyes moved down her back. She had fine blonde hairs that ran from the nape of her neck, to between the shoulder blades, and down to the top of her underwear, that was now pulled down because of her bent position over the sink, emphasising the crack between the cheeks of her bottom.

He quickly turned his attention back to her hair and finished rinsing, he felt discourteous looking at her body when she herself was at a disadvantage.

"I think that's enough, Ed, would you find a towel to put around my neck?"

In one swift movement she was standing up straight again, her hands tying the towel around her head, while she tried to focus on Copping through stinging eyes.

He gazed at Jocyline's body before finding her eyes on his. The picture of her slim, naked body lingered in his mind, but he had lost his desire and regained his composure.

Just as he began to feel relieved that he had survived the ordeal, things went from bad to worse. Directly in front of him, Jocyline changed her underwear and put on a new bra.

She laughed at him. "Come on, Ed, don't just stand there, go and put the kettle on, let's have a drink. I'll be with you once I'm dressed."

He stumbled from the bathroom and found the kettle, his hand trembling as he turned on the switch.

After a few minutes, she entered the room and was dressed in a rather conservative blouse, with a huge collar, that was pulled tight at the waist with a belt. She stared at him with those light blue eyes, and they looked mischievous as she pulled them away, gliding her tall figure over the carpet. She sat elegantly on the one of the plush armchairs, still saying nothing but continuing to stare at the Irishman.

He felt intimidated, perhaps she had expected more from him, but his mind was not on whether she was interested in him, but whether she was an informer, and he had felt susceptible throughout the whole incident.

Not a word was said for fifteen minutes, until finally Copping stood up, excused himself, and made for the door.

He turned to say goodbye, but she was already reading a magazine and did not even look up.

Chapter 33

A Different Type of Grass

Summer/Autumn 1986

Two days later.

As expected, Copping got a call from Mahmoud's secretary. He was grateful as he wanted to get this over with and make his way to Basra.

"Mr Copping, will you please attend Mr Mahmoud's office at 10 o'clock, he wants to have a half-hour meeting before you leave the office."

Sunday morning, 10:00 hrs.

Copping felt nervous as he sat waiting to be called in. He tried to remember the points that he was going to make, as he felt he needed to have excuses ready. Then, at ten past ten, the secretary asked him to go through.

Mahmoud looked greyer and older than the last time Copping had spoken with him. His head was down, and he was reading, so Copping waited until his boss looked up before being summoned to sit on the chair opposite his desk.

He had not yet spoken a word, and within a few moments, Alex Magarian the Armenian engineering manager entered the room. Magarian nodded to Copping and sat on a chair to the right of Mahmoud.

Copping thought the atmosphere was tense and expected something dramatic to be said. Magarian then turned to Mahmoud and asked, "Shall I call Sadr?"

Mahmoud looked up. "No! Our conversation should go no further then this room."

He quickly looked at Magarian, then to Copping, and returned his gaze to the paper he was reading. As Mahmoud flipped the paper forward, Copping recognised the stationary, it was from the command council.

"Gentleman there are two aspects on our agenda that need to be clarified quickly. Before the end of the week, the two of you will give me the answers, not 'maybes', not 'ifs', but confirmed answers."

A silence followed, and Mahmoud still remained transfixed on the paper, while the other two continued staring at him, waiting with anticipation.

"The first and most important point of our conversation is an answer to the letter that I have received directly from the command council, and I do not want to vague or false facts when I answer this in three days." There was a pause for maybe a minute, but for Copping it seemed longer.

"Both of you will visit the storage facilities for Project 109 tomorrow and report back to me here in three days. I sincerely hope that your report confirms that all work will be finished by the last day of November, which is in three weeks. I want a confirmation of what exceptions, if any, exist. This might include inspection certificates for construction and commissioning." He thought for a moment longer then added, "And that goes for all five projects."

He continued, "Mr Copping will make a presentation regarding the detail of work remaining, with any potential show-stoppers. And Mr Magarian, as the chief engineer, you will endorse this. I also want a detailed report of the contents of the bunker from you." And he nodded in Magarian's direction.

Both Magarian and Copping looked at each other and nodded, but Mahmoud never looked up, it was so unlike his normal jovial self. He only said, in a cold tone, "I might add, gentleman, that our very existence may rely on what you find, so don't let me down, and please shut the door when you leave."

A few minutes later, in Magarian's office, they both changed their itineraries for the week and discussed the travel and accommodation arrangements.

Copping was particularly relieved that nothing else was on his agenda, but he assumed that he would soon be busy after the hand-over of the construction works.

*****

A car with a driver picked Copping up at the Sheraton and he climbed in next to Magarian. Although Copping did not spend much time with the man he had come to know him well. He was born in Turkey to Armenian parents, who had fled the Armenian holocaust imposed by the Turks during the first war. It was reported at the time that 1.5 million Armenians were brutally murdered, although some managed to flee, like Magarian's parents, and move to Iraq where they settled. He went on to study hard at school and got his degree in London, where there was a large contingent of his fellow countrymen.

He was now a man in his late fifties, of slim build, and always wore a suit and tie. He had a lean and handsome face that rarely smiled, but when he did it lit up the room. He had a close relationship with his fellow countrymen around the world, with a special affiliation with the Armenian contingent in London. And over the next few days, Copping would find out even more about his chief engineer.

On the journey to the site, Magarian stuck with the rules and insisted that Copping wore a woollen hat pulled down over his eyes, although he had offered Copping various alternatives. Despite being slightly uncomfortable, Copping was happy regarding this covert approach to things.

However, this time the drive seemed to take longer than normal, and Copping was hot when he rolled off the blind and the car came to a stopped.

Magarian, with his handsome but serious face, addressed Copping as he emerged from his driving seat. "No Italian fortress for you tonight, Edward." He paused as he shut the car door. "Because we've been honoured to stay in the newly built accommodation block, and I'm sure you'll find it an improvement, even though it's built underground."

Copping understood but made no comment, as he thought almost anything would be an improvement from the previous accommodation.

They walked to the new site, and the work carried out by the North Koreans looked amazing. The roof was a reflection of the local countryside, with a real-life village built on the wave-shaped tiles, while the outside was disguised to appear rural with rocks, trees and ruins of small buildings.

After entering the reception area, they dressed in white overalls, boots, gloves and a mask. Walking to the lift, they started to descend, and the first few metres had a good view of the outside before it passed underground.

When departing the lift at minus two, the area they entered was in semi-darkness and the main lights came on after sensing their movements. The floor design looked complicated as it was corralled in different shapes and sizes. Every section had a mass of crates, drums and tanks, each with various labels attached, identifying dangerous goods and their storage instructions. The surroundings were pristine, as one would expect with explosives storage.

There were groups of Korean technicians working on cabling blocks, but were supervised by Europeans. The men looked to Copping as though they were Italian, or from one of the surrounding Mediterranean countries.

The bunker floor spaces were about thirty to forty percent full, stocked with various types of equipment. Copping strained his eyes to identify the contents, but checked himself, he might be seen acting suspiciously.

Most of the drums were labelled with a language he recognised, from a European source, and each had strict instructions on how they should be handled, and the positioned they would be stacked.

That evening, lying on his bed in the accommodation quarters of the storage bunker, Copping recounted what he had seen during the walk around.

He could not take photographs, so he had tried to memorise the labels on the containers. The description on some of the packages were familiar, these captions included Sarin, Tabun, Mycotoxin and Botulin Toxin. He would make sure to check the use and affect when he had time alone. He was already aware that nerve gas and germ warfare were all part of the weapons used in the war against both the Kurds and the Iranians.

He had also discovered forty tins of Yellow Cake that was to be used in the immediate process of uranium, along with long tubes that he suspected were linked to uranium enrichment.

He also noted a delivery address on one of drums, 'Al-Tuwaitha, Baghdad', and guessed these had be delivered to the main centre, then redirected. The description of the contents showed it was anthrax.

He had separated from Magarian earlier in the investigations, giving the excuse that it would be more affective if they separated and reviewed their findings together later on. However, for most of the time, a young Italian engineer showed him around, explaining the different storage methods.

He would have to meet up with Magarian later to discuss the outstanding construction and commissioning certification, but now his mind was full of information that he needed to memorise, and he did not dare to write any of it down.

Later in his room, his mind was so full, he soon fell asleep fully clothed on the bed, and did not wake until the morning.

He met Magarian after breakfast and together they checked drawings and related test certification for both the construction and commissioning work, all of which were detailed and meticulously prepared.

Copping then added his name to the certification that would allow the bunker to be handed over to the military.

They had met the command council's directive, but he still had to ensure everything was prepared for the work on the south Iraqi pipelines.

Chapter 34

A Growing Army

Autumn 1986

It turned out to be a busy and tiresome week, full of intense travelling. The dangers of being hit by military vehicles, or being blown up by land mines, left Copping in a very timorous state. The road from Baghdad to Basra was still classed as a battlefield, following Operation Dawn, so he was happy to safely spend a few more days on site without incident, and as a bonus he witnessed the Petroleum institute handing over the plant to the government.

As it was an official ceremony, he noticed that two members of the command council were present. Both seemed very sombre but one gave a seemingly power speech and it was greeted by loud applause from those present.

On the same day Project 109 was also handed over to the government, but only Mahmoud was in attendance, and he was reported to be very happy.

*****

Now all projects in total have been handed over to the government with the exception of some 'as built drawings, these will be complete before end of November"

Copping arrived on the morning of the 20th November 1986 he drove directly to the site and noticed the changes. The offices had recently moved, and the security had been stepped up and the army were now everywhere you looked.

In order to access the new compound, it was necessary to clear security, which was now more stringent and more forms to sign before admittance.

The presence of armed guards is always alarming, and in this case it was even more imposing, they were very diligent when checking the security passes, and did so without a smile, it was obvious the constructors were now not welcome on the site.

After three hours of talking, posturing and telephone calls back to his office in Baghdad, he was allowed access.

Copping had deduced that the unusual attendance of so much security was appropriate due to the alleged infiltration of a militia group member, which had been reported in a recent bulletin. It was apparent that a British truck driver travelling from Az Zubayr to London had been stopped at the border and arrested due to the possession of drugs found in his truck.

His subsequent interview disclosed that an undesirable agent was operating on the site. On this basis the Ba'ath party assumed rightly or wrongly that this person was a member of the Shia militia whom they knew operated in the area.

Copping immediately had his suspicions regarding the driver who had been carrying the box on site, as well as the car that sped by him whilst he was resting on the banks of the Shatt al Arab.

It all pointed to his friend Ismail, and even if it was, he still did not want to see him arrested, as he knew he would end up on the banks of the Tigris one Friday afternoon with a bullet in his head.

Copping then began to worry and went in search of Ismail. He found him talking to Robert Norris in the office, both were checking the recent modifications to the Umm Qsar pipeline. It was the last piece of the jigsaw, and the work was now virtually complete with only some minor changes outstanding.

"Can I suggest that we complete all aspects of the design quickly?"

Ismail smiled. "Of course, don't worry! It will be completed in a week." Ismail looked at Norris and they both nodded.

Norris was leaving the site and returning to London, so he collected his personal things, shook hands with both of them, and got in the taxi that was waiting for him outside the office.

Outside, with no one to overhear them, Copping opened the conversation that might end their friendship.

"Ismail, we have been good friends over the time of the project but we may now must say goodbye, and quickly."

Ismail shrugged, "Thank you, Ed. What are you trying to say?"

Copping relayed the story to his friend, and after he had finished an intense silence existed between them.

"You're saying that I'm in danger? But the party have nothing on me."

'They don't have to have anything on you, suspicion is enough."

"Are you saying I should find a place to hide, like a rat?"

Copping looked at the ground and shook his head.

It was now apparent that Copping's suspicions were correct. Ismail was in fact part of an Iraqi Shia militia group that opposed Saddam and the Ba'ath party, and had been peddling drugs to help support them.

"Have you anywhere to hide?"

"I have friends, but this will put the whole organisation in jeopardy, the houses here are often searched by the guard."

"You must drop all connections until this thing blows over and save yourself."

"And can I trust you, Ed? What if you're interrogated?"

"I can't say how I would react if tortured, but you can trust me under normal interrogation, and I'll not mention your name whilst I remain in Iraq."

They turned and walked back to the office, but the final words were spoken before they re-entered.

"I must go, the truck driver may have already named me, and I have no defence."

He looked at Copping and smiled. "You have my Kufiya, and I hope that it always reminds you of me and the friendship we had." His face became solemn as he stepped forward. He then hugged Copping warmly, turned, and disappeared through the door.

Copping followed Ismail in his car that evening as they passed the gate, and while the guard took their names and checked their papers. Then they both drove their separate ways.

Copping never found out how Ismail fared, but his scarf and headband remained in his possession as a fond memory of a good friend.

The next day.

Copping drove back to Baghdad, he took the route past the battlefield near to Al Qurna, during his drive he had the feeling he might be under scrutiny when he returned to the office, especially as most knew that he was friendly with Ismail.

Although, being a friend of a felon is not proof of guilt, he thought. *But it may be construed as having criminal intent.*

Copping made discreet enquiries regarding the Shia military and discovered that Ismail was part of the Badr Brigade, a Shia military group headed by Hadi al-Amiri. This organisation was formed in 1982 and continued to grow in numbers, becoming victorious in the fight against Saddam, the opposing Allied forces, and later they helped to defeat ISIS.

*****

Mahmoud's secretary did not smile when Copping approached her desk the next day. She had asked him to attend a meeting with Mahmoud and he was nervous, still unsure as to why he had been summoned. When he reached her desk, she asked him to go through to his office.

For a few moments Mahmoud did not say a word, he only continued writing at his desk. Sadr was already seated in the chair next to him and was just staring at the floor, giving nothing away.

Suddenly Mahmoud looked up. "Mr Copping, there are three things that I need to make clear immediately. The first is a success story. I congratulate you in assisting directly with

Project 109, it has been an amazing success so far, and the work carried out by the Italians and the Koreans has been excellent. Your team here in Baghdad have been superb, and as you have been a valued member, I congratulate you. The second point is the mess up of the design of pipework at Umm Qsar, although completed on time it was an unwanted problem.

"The third, and arguably most important item on our agenda, is the treasonable action by one of our staff, and because of its importance, I need a report from you regarding your connection with Ismail." He paused, allowing Copping to process everything he had just said.

"Please explain to me your association with this man, and after you leave here, you will need to write a report to the party's intelligence section."

Copping looked straight into Mahmoud's eyes, holding his gaze steady.

"I knew nothing of Ismail leaving his post until this morning. He was my friend, and I spoke with him in detail regarding the work at Umm Qsar, but nothing more."

"Did you know that he was part of the Iranian militia?" Mahmoud was aggressive.

"Mr Mahmoud, no! That was never the case!" Copping lied.

Copping went on, "I had a long talk with him regarding the re-design work and he has been organising the workforce. He then duly informed me that the 'as built' drawings will be completed in a week, and that was the last time we spoke." He paused, trying to remain calm.

"Since then, I was shocked to hear that he may be part of a Shia militia. He was a friend, and I liked him, but I would not cover for him in such treasonable circumstances."

Mahmoud and Sadr did not say a word for a while, then Mahmoud looked at him and changed the subject to the work that Steve Plant should have carried out.

"Oh yes, sir, the design work is completed and has been accepted by the client. As I said, the 'as built' drawings will be completed in a week."

"OK, Mr Copping, this all seems fine, but please be aware that this business may not go away for some time, so be on your toes. In the meantime, make sure everything is handed over.

"And please shut the door when you leave, I need to speak with Sadr."

Chapter 35

A Turn-up for the Books

Autumn 1986

The last few days for Copping had been hectic, and the situation with Ismail had been disastrous for him. At best, the petroleum company will only review Copping's contract, but should party intelligence refute his story, they could jail him. For now, he could only wait, and that was the worst part.

On Thursday, after the meeting with Mahmoud, he stayed close to the hotel as he guessed he would be followed by intelligence if he went far. So he met up with JP at the bar, but decided not to mention anything about the incident with Ismail.

*****

On Friday the television was jammed with information concerning consecutive battles with the Kurds and the Iranians, who were once again breaching the boundaries of the capital. As a result, people were getting concerned and the hotels were emptying fast.

Copping decided to stay in his hotel room for two days over Friday and Saturday, and return to the house on Monday evening as Leila had promised to visit him.

This thought normally excited him, but there were now extenuating circumstances, and he might have to move quickly should a warrant go out for his arrest. At this moment, Copping could feel his life crumbling.

Then, out of the blue, his hotel door buzzer sounded. Copping approached it with extreme caution. And there, standing in front of him, was Jocyline, dressed to the hilt. Next to her was a man carrying a camera, covered with desert dust.

"Can we come in, Ed? We'd like a word."

Copping looked closely at this tall, leggy American who when he had last seen her was naked in front of him, causing that image of her to run through his mind. He could not come to terms with his reluctance to take her, but now it was a different scenario and he waited to see what she wanted.

"I have come to say goodbye, but before I do, let me introduce you to a friend of mine from my school days."

"My name is Criff," said her partner, making the introduction himself.

He continued, "I've been working with Jenny for the past few weeks, in the consular section of the US embassy."

Copping detected a faint accent, but he did not ask questions, and they shook hands.

Jocyline then turned to him. "Look, Ed, I can only stay for a coffee and then I must dash to the airport in case they close it and I'm left stranded." She seemed anxious.

"Why is there more turmoil with the war now?" Copping asked, while they all made themselves comfortable on available chairs in the room.

Criff seemed to know what was going on and explained that the Iranians had created a new front, amassing 600,000 troops at the border.

"I'm expecting an attack shortly, and I'm sure Saddam will have an answer," Criff added.

"That's a massive force." Copping was amazed at the number.

"Listen, Edward, I'll be staying in Baghdad for a while and have been sent here to establish what construction projects the Iraqis are currently involved in." He glanced up at Copping to see his reaction before continuing. "My main interest is purely technical, and I'm especially interested in the concrete structures being built. You know, like the material mix and curing time."

Copping thought to himself, *Is this man serious? I should end this session quickly, but for the sake of my own safety I'll keep it going until I find an excuse to end it.*

Jocyline brought the coffees over and the trio did not speak for a few minutes. Copping found the silence excruciating.

"I haven't a clue, not being a civil engineer myself. I'm afraid I can't help you on this occasion."

Criff said nothing and just looked up at the ceiling, his attitude suggested he was annoyed with such a vague answer.

"Oh, well that's too bad, Edward, as I need this to complete my report."

He paused. "Perhaps you could find out for me... just between us, and if you need say some reimbursement, then I can do that too."

Copping could not believe what he was hearing and slowly stood up to address Jocyline. "I think it's time to go, Jenny. I have a very important meeting to get to. I hope we meet again." He stopped and moved to give her a hug.

"Absolutely, Ed," she replied, and they hugged before she made her way to the door.

"Well, yes. Me too," said Criff, who rose quickly to join Jocyline. He then shook hands with Copping, and without saying another word, left the room.

*****

Copping found himself deep in thought and kept trying to place the slight accent he had detected when Criff spoke. He was starting to become quite paranoid about it, so decided to get out of his hotel room and have a drink at the bar.

He was pleased to meet JP, but also mockingly wondered if JP was ever anywhere else.

"What are you having today, Ed?" JP asked, in his usual cool tongue.

"A beer please, oh and before I forget, I want to ask your advice regarding an accent I've just heard. It's one that I can't seem to place, it's almost American, but with a light sort of tinge on the emphasised syllables." Copping seemed tied up in his explanation.

"That doesn't give me much to go on, but I did see a guy leaving with Jenny, so I'd hazard a guess that his was an Israeli accent."

"What has that got to do with Jenny?"

"Well, I've met her before at a meeting and found that she is from a Jewish American family, so I suspect she is either working for Mossad or the CIA." He paused. "Or both."

After a few more drinks, Copping said goodnight to JP and returned to his room. Much to his surprise, he fell onto his bed and slept soundly, even though he had a lot on his mind.

The safe house, Sunday.

That morning, Copping picked Leila up from outside of the British club, as she had wanted to visit his house in Az Zubayr for some time. This visit was planned a week in advance, giving him time to hire a band of cleaners that swept through the place, and it looked amazing when they had finished.

Things were quiet at work, allowing him to arrange a few days off to spend some time with Leila. As he was on his way to pick her up, he realised he did not know where she lived or what she did for a living.

In reality, it was a meeting of convenience for them, so there were no coffees or aperitifs when they arrived. There was only a few minutes of calm before their eyes met, then in an instant they were frolicking on the settee. They then fell onto the floor, with no hesitation or interruption, and they made the most of their private afternoon.

Later that day.

Leila wandered around the house while Copping watched some television in the library. She enjoyed the house's expanse and the many rooms, but none more so than his bedroom.

The weather outside was cold, with the wind coming from the north west, making it feel ten degrees lower than it was.

Although it was cold outside, he still did not need much persuading to join Leila, who was sprawled out in the large bed. And it wasn't long before they kicked off the duvet, as the temperature between them had suddenly risen.

However, their peaceful day was interrupted when the house phone rang, a phone that Copping had never used before. "Hi Edward, its Criff. I rang you at work with no joy, so I thought I'd try here."

"How did you get both my work and this number, Criff? I never use either."

"Never thought of it, Edward, just asked Jenny for your contact details before she left."

"OK Criff, how can I help?" Criff was about to respond, before Copping added, "But I must inform you, I didn't go to the office today."

"No, that's fine, it was just a reminder. I'll try you again later."

Copping shivered, he knew this man was going to be a problem.

He returned to Leila, who was sitting snugly on the settee, with her legs pulled up to her chin and her eyes on the television. "Anything important, Ed?"

Copping shook his head, but it was some time before he could get Criff off of his mind.

Chapter 36

Tailing Off

November 1986

Now that Jocyline had being relocated, the meeting with Criff was not of interest, and Copping was not looking forward to hearing from him again.

In the office, Sadr was his normal self, just sitting at his desk and occasionally making tea. Although it seemed as if nothing had changed, Copping sensed a quietness that unnerved him. Things were not normal. So he decided it would be best if he got out of the office and started making arrangements to travel. He packed extra food to ensure he did not get a bad stomach, then filled the car with petrol, putting a spare jerrycan in the boot, to ensure he had a contingency plan in the event of a hold up or any other unexpected problems.

Copping intended to stay just three days and hoped that the work at Umm Qsar would be virtually finished by the time he got back. Then, just before he was about to leave, he got a call from Magarian who informed him that both highways were under attack by long range missiles from the Iranians, and it was unwise to travel unless accompanied. So he cancelled his trip, returned to the office, and moped around with little to do.

Two weeks later – Baghdad

The chief engineer informed Copping that all drawing work was finished on the 27th November 1986, and oil was expected to be pumped through over the next few days. The site foreman then advised him that all test certification was completed, and the dossiers had already been sent to Mahmoud.

This lifted the mood in the office, and just after lunch, Mahmoud's secretary brought over an invite. Mahmoud was calling a general meeting to celebrate the completion of the project.

Copping found himself in tentative mood as he sipped a lemon cordial in the hall, smiling and having general chit-chat with the people that he knew spoke English. Then, out of the blue, Mahmoud beckoned him over, gave him a warm handshake and made a joke. It was complicated, but he laughed anyway, even though he did not understand what it was about.

Copping had never seen Mahmoud so happy, and at one point he thought he might get offered more work, but nothing was said.

Copping realised if nothing was forthcoming, he would have to make plans for moving on. He had pencilled both Turkey and Australia as possibilities, but Turkey could be reached by road, making it the easier and most suitable option. Australia would need more extensive research, but the best option for a long haul would be to pay a cargo passenger captain to take him.

One week later – Early December 1986

Since the completion of the project nothing positive, or of any interest, had happened in Copping's life. He thought of contacting Patten, but then he did not expect any favours as he held no responsibility for Copping, his contract was with Mahmoud.

Switching between different channels of the television did not help either, as only a few were in English. In the end, he settled for CNN to find out news from the west.

Then the telephone rang, which was a surprise as it seemed that his popularity had waned given that he hadn't spoken with anyone for over a week, especially now that JP was on leave for a month.

Copping tentatively picked up the phone. "Hello?"

"Edward? It's me, Safiya."

Chapter 37

A Desperate Time

"Edward, you need to help me, my life is falling apart! I was taken off of my normal hospital duties and sent to places too horrible to mention, and now I'm on house arrest!" She tried to take a deep breath. "I've left my apartment without permission and I only have a few moments to talk."

"Where are you, Safiya?"

"I am in hospital accommodation on a temporary basis, but you have to get me out. We can make it to Damascus, then at least I'll be safe for a time."

"But I need travel documents, I need to clear funds…" He had started stammering. "There's so much to do."

She was almost in tears. "Let's take a chance and just go, Edward. I have money and so do you, we can use that and claim asylum wherever we go."

He was taken aback. He so desperately wanted to help her, but his careful disposition made him hesitate.

"Please, Edward, come now, please! Pick me up at the end of Rashid Street, before the intersection with Macktoum street, in one hour." Her voice was excited.

"You've got to give me time, Safiya!"

"Edward, I haven't got any more time. I'll see you in one hour." And the line went dead.

He slumped into a chair and tried to process her demand. What she suggested was preposterous, they would be shot on site. It would be madness to flee now, they had better to wait and give themselves time to plan.

They would be running on instinct, and that is only if they made it across a border. Even if they were not caught in Iraq, they still could be incarcerated in whatever country they chose to enter.

The best border would be Jordan, as Syria would almost certainly end up with arrest, and Iran and Saudi Arabia were not options.

He continued to rack his brains. Perhaps, in time, the best route might be through Kurdistan, although the area was saturated with tribesman, this may be detrimental to Safiya.

His mind was in turmoil and time was passing fast. He could not think of a solution, and to pick her up without a plan or adequate funding would be madness.

He had other thoughts too, like what if she had been coerced by the secret police or the army to trap him? They knew she was a dissident with no respect for the Iraq authority, and they may have offered her a way out if she handed him over.

One hour and twenty minutes later.

Copping was still in his hotel room when the telephone rang out again. He felt incredibly uncomfortable and dreaded answering it. He reached for receiver, not knowing how to explain himself in this situation.

Her voice was more animated than usual. "Edward, you know how a female in my country cannot be seen waiting around alone on the roadside, and yet I'm still waiting for you! Where are you? I feel so vulnerable with all these people staring at me while I wait for you! When are you coming?"

He felt so ashamed and explained that he wanted more time, they both would not get far without a well-thought-out plan.

The phone was silent, and he could hear her breathing, but she said nothing.

"Edward, I must go, it's a hopeless situation. Hopefully I'll be able to contact you soon." And with that, the line went dead. Copping held onto the receiver for some time, feeling useless, unwanted and disloyal, as another piece of his life crumbled before him!

The following Tuesday.

Copping was at the petroleum institute looking at the newly proposed pipeline, studying a drawing from Kirkuk in the north. The pipeline would pass through Turkey to the Mediterranean, and Copping was hoping that this could be his next job.

The phone on his desk sounded and his secretary told him that Mr Patten was on the line for him from London.

"Copping, I've asked Iona to book you a flight back to London in the next forty-eight hours, she'll confirm the details with you. Please don't mention this to any of your business colleagues though, I'll notify Maliki once you're in the air."

'You realise I'm on local hire, Tom, and that I'll need a visa to leave."

"All done, I arranged this two months ago when the war started to become a threat to you. It'll not be a safe place for an Irishman if the Iranians break through, is that clear?"

"OK then, will I arrange the transport from here to the airport?"

"No, we'll arrange everything and send you your itinerary. So, get packed up and be ready to go. It's a morning flight and we'll be getting you to the airport very early. Do you have you any questions?"

"No, Tom."

"OK, but remember you're on your own once you touch down in England."

"Thanks Tom, I'll come visit you in Paddington."

"That's fine." And they both hung up.

Patten then picked the phone back up and dialled a protected number. It rang a few times and then, "Webster here."

"Yes, Mr Webster, just to inform you…"

Chapter 38

Baghdad in the Morning Sun

Tuesday morning, 04:00 hrs.

When the alarm woke Copping, the first thought that came into his mind was Michael O'Byrne. He had never forgotten that he was the one that could trigger his demise by reporting him to the Special Intelligence Services in London and get him picked up when he landed at Heathrow. Hopefully he would not find out and that would give Copping time to disappear. He had his savings from Iraq and would have access to previous funds stored in the UK, so it would give him time to get organised once he was free of the airport.

It had been six years since Copping had left the UK as Barney Coughlin, and he was hoping things were now quiet.

He jumped out of bed and shivered, as the air was surprisingly cold. He hurried himself into the shower and began dressing for the journey back to the UK.

It was still dark outside and very quiet as Copping departed the house. He walked through the streets to a meeting point where he agreed to be picked up and sure enough, at exactly five o'clock, the noise of an approaching taxi broke the silence.

The journey seemed quick, and he was surprised to find that the departure check-in was already open so early in the morning. Although, there was only one kiosk with a border officer was operating, and there were only a few other passengers walking around.

He handed his passport, ticket, and visa to the officer for scrutiny. Whilst this was going on, the screech of brakes could be heard as a car pulled up outside, and he could see it's lights turn off as some officers left the vehicle. Copping was not impressed but knew better than to make a comment, and returned to his business of checking in.

The border control officer turned to him and made an excuse in broken English. "I'm sorry sir, but you will have to wait a few minutes, our special forces officers need to speak with you."

Copping was about to ask why when two men blocked his path out of the airport, and two blocked the way he had come in.

One of them held his police identification in one hand, the other held Copping's passport high and said, "Mr Copping, you'll need to come with us to our headquarters to answer some questions."

"But I have to catch a flight to Heathrow."

"As I said, sir, you must come with us."

As he was heading towards the car, he passed his friend Wally Wright, the cricketer, who shouted his greetings. Then Wright, noticing the escort, redirected his gaze, and cut off any contact with his former friend.

The journey back to the capital was frightening; the special Iraqi police team who were all very serious were driving him. They sat in silence for the entire journey.

Copping began to panic. What was this arrest all about? Surely it could not be anything to do with O'Byrne, or the episode with his friend Ismail.

At the station he was put in a cell and told by an officer with limited English that he would be questioned at ten o'clock, when his commanding officer came in.

In the cell, two other men were talking in a language not familiar to Copping. They looked civilised and once in the cell, the two practically ignored him.

He was the last of the three to be questioned, but eventually he was brought from the cell to a glass panelled room in the corridor, adjacent to the cells.

Walking along the corridor, he passed the other inmates, and the inhabitants looked anxious.

He was then kept waiting for over an hour, before the two men that had arrested him sat on either side of him in silence.

Then the senior officer arrived, and Copping was brought before him.

"Mr Edward Copping, you have been under surveillance for some time, and I find it necessary to arrest you under suspicion of breaking our international confidentiality policy."

He went on, "You'll be retained under guard until your case comes to court."

Copping was going to protest but thought it best not to say anything. The officer looked tired and irritable.

He was led back to his cell, until later during the day when he was taken to a detention centre just out of the city and told he would remain there until his case came to court.

The situation remained the same for four months, and so he requested to see the Irish consulate representative. He felt it was a human rights case if a person was held in a foreign jail without charge, but this obviously fell on deaf ears.

Maliki was duly informed, and he advised Patten in London of the situation. All of this information was then passed onto the Irish authorities, but then nothing.

Copping was never an employee of Patten's. Whilst he worked in Iraq, he was a local employee of the Petroleum Institute, and in Europe he was an Irish national and a wanted man. He began to wander whether the Irish authorities or MI6 were involved in this.

However, he had been a key person in Iraq, directly involved in successful construction work, and Patten had a certain loyalty to him.

A few weeks after he heard of Copping's demise, he wrote a letter to the Irishman assuring him of his support, but at the same time explaining the difficult situation due to his own connection with Webster and his M6 operation.

He added that he had passed the details of all his good work to the Irish authorities, and he attached a note received from the two power plant engineers who arrived at the safe house the very morning Copping had left for the airport.

A note from Alistair. (Power plant service engineer.)

Dear Mr Patten,

We have just heard, with some surprise, that the Iraqi authorities in Baghdad have detained Ed Copping. This information was given to us by word of mouth, and we do not know the true reasons as to why this was necessary.

As you know, my colleague and I periodically visit Iraq to service the power plant that we installed in Mosul last year. It was during one of these visits that we arrived at the safe house at about 09:30 a.m. and Ed had already left for the airport. It was unfortunate, as we would have liked to have seen him, whenever we mixed in the past it was good fun and his company would have cheered us up after the long flight. It was about an hour later that I answered the phone to a lady who became distraught when I explained that Ed had already left for the airport. Whether she was doubtful of what I had told her, or if she was desperate to see him, I don't know. She then asked me if I could phone him and advise him that she would take a taxi and meet him at the airport, and I told her that his flight would have already departed and she started to sob. I then asked her if there was anything that I could do to help, and she said it was too late and put the phone down. She never rang again, but I think she said her name was Safi or Safiya.

If there is anything that I can help with, please do not hesitate to contact either of us.

Regards,
Alistair Roberts

Six months later, 16th April 1987.

Edward Copping was taken to court without warning and without legal defence representation. The charge of treason were read out by the prosecutor and Copping was sentenced to twenty years in prison. No specific details or reasons for the arrest were stated, and his protestations fell on deaf ears. He was led away in tears of frustration and despair.

1988–2003.

In 1998, a ceasefire of the war between Iraq and Iran was brokered by the United Nations under Resolution 598.

Then, in 1990, operation 'Desert Storm' transpired when the United States attacked the holding forces in Kuwait, freeing them from Iraqi occupation. It was the start of the Persian war and the hostilities included the Gulf war and the Iraq war, of which the latter included the bombing of Iraq by their allies. It was end of the Ba'ath party reign and was followed with the execution of Saddam Hussein.

There was trepidation by the allies regarding the legality of the attacks, but it nevertheless went ahead on the basis that Saddam had weapons of mass destruction, although the inspectors claimed there were none.

David Kelly was a British scientist, who specialised in biological warfare, and acted as one of the leaders of the inspection team that visited Iraq. In July 2003, he had informed a BBC reporter, Andrew Gilligan, that the Iraqi weapons of mass destruction could be mobilised within forty-five minutes. Gilligan then reported this information on a BBC Radio 4 programme, after which, Kelly refused to take sole responsibility as the leak.

It was known that weapons of this kind would be the critical factor in legalising an attack on Iraq, and so the allies, based on flawed information, now had a legal reason to start preparing an attack on Baghdad.

In July 2003, Kelly was then told that he must appear in front of the Intelligence and Security and Foreign Affairs Select committees to discuss the leaked information. The day after his final appearance in court, Kelly was found dead a mile from his home, and despite contradictory evidence, it was reported as a suicide.

President Bush and Prime Minister Blair now had the legality to invade and bomb Iraq. Unbeknown to Blair and Bush, Saddam Hussein did not possess weapons of mass destruction, and so Iraq was bombed, killing thousands of innocent Iraqi people. Later, the country was left in total disarray, with little power, sewer leakage and disease. ISIS tried to take over from the ruins that the allies had left behind, but local militia fought back and Iraq were the first Arab country to finally overcome them.

A month after Kelly's death, the UK government were subsequently accused of misrepresentation but were later cleared by the Hutton enquiry in August 2003.

*****

It would be a nice thought if Ismail, who absconded from the site where Ed Copping worked, joined the BAKR militia or later the Mehdi army, and survived to see Iraq's freedom from Saddam Hussein, and then, as a bonus, overcome the control of Isis. But the cost for this freedom was not cheap, and Iraq had to pay with the lives of too many of its people.

Chapter 39

Forever an Optimist

During his incarceration in an Iraqi jail, Copping had plenty of time to recall his recent life and the possible reasons behind his latest apprehension. He had, over the last six years, avoided capture by various authorities, even coming perilously close to being apprehended whilst in Zambia. And now, after such a successful period in Iraq, he had ended up in jail and he wanted to know why.

He continually filtered through people that could have betrayed him, while also considering a case of mistaken identity. After all, his look alike, Wally Wright, did pass him at the airport at the same time, on the same date.

His negative thoughts made him paranoid, and he started to make a mental list of the people that could have exposed him to this life of hell. He became obsessed with finding the answer, and although it did him no good, it gave him some comfort to know who was not to be trusted.

When he received the note from Patten, with the report from Alistair, the contents made him weep. It might have been better if he had run away with Safiya when he had the chance. He had his doubts regarding Safiya, but now he was paying for the doubt, and he felt he had betrayed her.

Her last telephone call made him think hard, he was transfixed for hours just remembering her last words, and after a while he put his head to his chest and sobbed.

While his list of all the possible candidates who may have betrayed him contained everyone he knew, it was needless to say that her name was at the bottom.

Michael O'Byrne
He was always a threat to Copping and he never found out what the IRA thought of O'Byrne's transgression to the KGB. That is, if he was even working with them at all. O'Byrne

certainly did not want information about himself spread throughout the world and he must have thought this was a possibility with Copping returning to the UK.

He would always be at the top of his list, as he was a man without principles.

George Mwanza

It was a concern of Copping's that Mwanza's purpose in life was to take money from the highest bidder, without any thought of loyalty. He was always looking for opportunities and took anything that came his way.

Why was he always in the right place when Copping wanted him? It was just too much of a coincidence.

JP (Jean Paul Krull)

JP was a good friend but Copping could never find out what JP did for a living, or what he did with the information he heard from visitors. It always seemed more than a pastime. The visit to his Italian friend was just at the right time, when a visa was required for a certain new envoy to the Vatican. That new envoy would slot in nicely to assist with the purchase of Yellow Cake from Niger, a project that was very possibly executed by the Italian mafia, and he was at Vincenso's house when the call came in.

It was his special talent to speak so many languages, and yet he never wanted anyone else other than Copping to know he spoke Arabic so fluently. Why?

Sadr

He was a real Ba'ath party member and may not have wanted Copping to return with detrimental thoughts on the Iraqi policies. So, perhaps he ensured that Copping would be grilled sometime in the future by one of the unfriendly intelligent services.

Copping thought of him as a friend, but it was Sadr's job to listen. Therefore, was it a coincidence that Copping was interrogated a short time after he disclosed his relationship with Safiya?

Alex Magarian
Magarian was an aloof man who strenuously protected his heritage and may have believed that Copping was guilty of passing classified information to his London office.

Copping felt that Magarian thought of him as a foreigner who was trying to upstage him. It is sometimes the quiet, studious people that are the most dangerous, and Magarian was this type of man. There was always a sense that he was hiding something that Copping could expose.

George Webster
The director of the SIS and an old foe, had failed for over six years in his bid to apprehend Copping. There are many ways to catch a thief, and Webster was clever enough to have set this up, as well as having the tools to do it. It would also be the cleanest way to do it, but he would need to know when he was leaving, and the one person who knew this was Patten.

Tom Patten
Patten told him how and when to leave, and he arranged the taxi. He also managed to get a ticket that had to be checked by one border officer who was on duty far earlier than necessary. This was making a strong case that Patten and Webster were in on this together.

Mr Mahmoud
While Mr Mahmoud was a fantastic man, who Copping kept in high esteem, the Command Council may have given him an order that he could not refuse. Worse still, Mahmoud may also have agreed the time and date that Copping could be demobilised and could have been an active part in his demise.

He thought he may be becoming paranoid over this situation, but things were beginning to make sense. The only way he may get out of this place was if the Ba'ath party ever went into administration. Which he knew to be a hopeless thought, one of despair.

The driver with the bag
The driver may have surrendered information to the secret police after he was apprehended on the Iraq border, but that will never be known. Worse still he may well have given a lot more information away if he was tortured.

That aspect will never be clarified.

Jenny Jocyline
An intriguing, enchanting and very dangerous woman. One who should not be underestimated, and it is possible that she may have been a joint agent for both the CIA and Mossad.

It's also possible that she informed Criff regarding the work that Copping was carrying out, without knowing the specific details.

Leila
A delightful young Kurdish lady, but as such she could have been trying to obtain information on the Iraqi military. This could be troop movements around Baghdad, gunnery positions, or exact locations of government offices.

While Copping considered that this may be the case, he knew it most likely was not true as she never gave the slightest inclination.

Ismail
While he is a doubtful contender, anyone involved in drugs can never be trusted. However, he had never given Ismail a reason to expose him or set him up for imprisonment.

Wally Wright
He thought Wally a friend but what was he doing at the airport the same time as he was arrested, and he snubbed him when he realised the police had arrested him.

Criff
He was a dangerous Mossad agent, working for a country constantly under threat from other Arab countries. He also never got what he wanted from Copping and may have felt that he needed to be taught a lesson.

Safiya
Perhaps she had succumbed to interrogation and was forced to phone Copping with her proposal. But to consider this after having read Alistair's letter, alongside his own memories of her, that is not an option.

Epilogue

This episode in history depicts Saddam Hussein as an egotistical warmonger and a cold-blooded killer, with a hatred for the Shia Muslim. If Saddam had made concessions during his reign, instead of fighting on blindly, the outcome could have changed history.

With a country at war, battles are won and lost by the numbers, and it did not help Iraq's cause when over half the population were Shia Muslim and did not want to fight. In fact, with the Shia militia operating in the south reversed the situation and strengthened Iran war effort.

By downgrading the Shia community, Saddam made his own goals more difficult and added to his growing list of enemies.

Time and again, wars are being lost because the timing of proceedings is not thought out systematically. If Saddam had nurtured his dreams and waited for the oil prices to rise, and his nuclear process developed longer he would have had developed the weapons that he was so close to getting, but his impatience finished him.

However, that being said, security and peace within Iraq never could have existed if he had been successful in his development of nuclear warheads. And that is only if he had protected his borders more rigorously and his scientists more personally.

His egotistical character also had misgivings, making enemies with neighbours that could have made a difference. If only he had offered them a handshake, instead of a clenched fist.

The world does not want leaders that can only protect life through war, and it is a better world now that another despot is removed from his throne of power. Unfortunately, another will take his place and the world will have to deal with them in the same way.

*****

Ed Copping was incarcerated for almost six years, and he became older and more emancipated as time went on. He received mail from his mother and his old friend Declan from Rostrevor, and was kept informed of the peace process. Then, on the 10th April 1998, the Good Friday agreement was signed and soon after, all IRA prisoners held by the British Government were freed. However, Ed Copping, formerly known as Barney Coughlin, did not qualify for freedom in Iraq.

Later, on the 17th January 2003, the American and British armed forces bombed Baghdad in the Iraq war, and the jailers in prison sympathetically freed all foreign prisoners.

Barney Coughlin was the last to leave the old concrete prison. As he emerged from its curved roof, he stopped while silhouetted against a city on fire, and raised his arms in defiance, following those before him.

Many tales have since been reported regarding sightings of Barney Coughlin, but nothing has been confirmed. The world may never know what became of him, whether he stayed and sought out Safiya, or whether she perished in the chaos of war.

Although, a map was found in Ed Copping's hotel room after he vacated it, and a line had been drawn from Baghdad to Damascus that included co-ordinates of a planned route, with times and expected vehicle speeds.

This map is now probably with the same collection of maps that Copping made of the expected missile drops, in the SIS archives.

A Coffee House in Zubayr

Glossary of Abbreviations

Saddam -	*Saddam Hussein*
GDP -	*Gross Domestic Profit*
b.p.d -	*Barrels per day (Oil Production rate)*
De Braun -	*WW2 German missile designer*
Becky Anderson -	*CNN news reader*
Knesset -	*Israeli Parliament (Unicameral national legislation of Israel)*
MIG -	*Russian-built fighter aircraft*
T-72 -	*Russian-built battle tank*
WMD -	*Weapons of mass destruction*
M16 -	*UK intelligence service (Overseas)*
MI5 -	*UK Intelligence service (UK)*
SIS -	*Secret Intelligence service*
MOSSAD -	*Israeli Secret Intelligence & security service*
HWASONG-5	*North Korean ballistic missile*
DON-	*In the Mafia crime hierarchy the DON is head of the family*
Strafed -	*Attack from aircraft using bombs/Machine gun fire*
SCUD -	*A type of long-range surface to surface missile*
IRA/PIRA -	*A paramilitary organisation claimed to descend from the organisation that in 1922 wanted to break with British rule*
IED -	*Improvised Explosive device A bomb fabricated in an improvised manner to make the worst damage.*

About the Author

Brian Godfrey was born and bred in an east Hertfordshire village called Stanstead Abbotts. During his boyhood he enjoyed the lazy summers, by fishing in the rivers and playing cricket with a bald tennis ball and a bat cut from flat timber.

During the winter months his pastimes were playing football and touch rugby on the hard tarmac roads, disturbed only at infrequent times by passing traffic.

But with play comes work and he went to school locally and later during his apprenticeship attended technical colleges at Welwyn and later Hatfield.

He went to sea as a junior engineer, soon establishing himself as a shift charge engineer and during his 'Ticket' break was offered work onshore as a watch engineer on a rig designed to test Nuclear submarine equipment.

In the seventies some opportunities became available for suitably trained personnel in the growing offshore industry and this work subsequently took him around the world.

In retirement he promised himself, he would write a trilogy; it would be inspired by a true story, although the names would change to protect the innocent; this is the final episode!

He has four grown up children and lives with his wife in Bishops Stortford; his final book of the trilogy will be issued in mid September 2021.

The trilogy is called 'The Cause'

Brian Godfrey
July 2021

Each book was sequentially issued:
'The Compassionate Terrorist' - 2016 – published by Matador
'Umtata' - 2020' – published by Matador
'A Guest House in AZ Zubayr' - 2021 – published by New Generation